YORK NOTES

General Editors: Professor A.N. Jeffares (*University of Stirling*) & Professor Suheil Bushrui (*American University of Beirut*)

KT-502-878

Thomas Hardy

JUDE THE OBSCURE

Notes by Margaret Stonyk

BA (ADELAIDE), PH D (LEEDS)

LONGMAN
YORK PRESS

YORK PRESS
Immeuble Esseily, Place Riad Solh, Beirut.

LONGMAN GROUP UK LIMITED
Longman House, Burnt Mill, Harlow,
Essex CM20 2JE, England
Associated companies, branches and representatives
throughout the world

First published 1980
Fifth impression 1990

ISBN 0-582-78126-4

Produced by Longman Group (FE) Ltd.
Printed in Hong Kong

Contents

Part 1

Introduction

The life of Thomas Hardy

In certain significant ways, the life of Thomas Hardy reads like the story of Jude Fawley softened and given a relatively happy ending. Hardy appears to be writing his final novel to trace the growth of his personal outlook: his view of an indifferent universe, human hopes ruined by the laws of chance, and his own battle with the class structure of English society. Like Jude, he felt that unnecessary obstacles had been placed in his way as he sought an education and emotional fulfilment. Of course, Hardy is not Jude, but Jude's tragic conflict with his circumstances is based on Hardy's more successful struggle. The character of Jude grows out of earlier literature to some degree, in particular Gray's famous 'Elegy Written in a Country Churchyard' of 1750, where the poet ponders how many potentially great men have been condemned by their obscure birth to mean lives. But there is much in Jude Fawley that is also Thomas Hardy, and we seem to see Hardy asking himself what caused Jude to fail when Thomas, similarly ambitious and gifted, became a rich and famous writer who was to be buried in Westminster Abbey among the great poets of his country.

Hardy was born in 1840 in the village of Bockhampton in the county of Dorset, which becomes Jude's native 'Mellstock' in the fictional county of 'Wessex'. His father was a builder and mason like Jude, but successful enough to employ his own labourers. Nevertheless Hardy felt the contempt of the 'genteel' classes for his relatively humble origins and writes his resentment into the character of Jude who is prevented from going to university because he works with his hands. Hardy's consciousness that he was not, strictly speaking, a 'gentleman' affected him profoundly and clouded his life, yet his status midway between the middle class and the peasantry gave him an invaluable understanding of a wide cross-section of English life. A gentleman might have written sentimentally about the destruction of picturesque rural traditions; Hardy may share this regret from time to time, but he is wryly aware of the miseries behind the charm of the countryside. He had seen two public hangings as a boy and knew of cases of illegitimacy, suicide, incest and the horrors of the workhouse; the darker side of rural simplicity. The famous description of the casual and joyless promiscuity of the villagers in *Jude the Obscure* is written by someone who watched such behaviour as a member of village society and not as an outsider protected by his rank. Hardy can see that a life lived among ideas in the city can perhaps be richer and fuller than the mean jealousies of a decaying village. Yet he regrets that the ties to old roots stretching down into unrecorded history are breaking and people move through a changed world without families or traditions to support them. In most of Hardy's novels a countryman is threatened by 'the modern vice of unrest' in the shape of a city-educated woman who robs him of his old certainties and then rejects him. Sue and Jude form such a pair.

As a child, Hardy was 'ecstatic' or imaginative and excitable like the young Jude who seems 'to see things in the air'. He used to play at being a clergyman, and his novels show that this taste for moral persuasion continued into adult life. He was lucky to go to a school which taught Latin, one of the requirements for university entrance, for the boy already had the ambitions of a scholar. At the age of fifteen he was apprenticed by his family to a local architect so that he could rise in the world through a respectable profession, but the boy got up early every morning to teach himself Greek for the Cambridge entrance examination.

Hardy's work with an employer who specialised in the fashionable 'Gothic revival' style, which built new churches after medieval models and secular buildings which looked like churches, comes in for satirical treatment in *Jude the Obscure*. The 'Gothic revival' in architecture, an inescapable feature of nineteenth-century art, which left its mark over the countryside and the cities, is the central symbol for Hardy of a religion which has forgotten the spirit which began it. We see this aesthetic phenomenon today as an interesting if misguided attempt to recapture the artistic and moral strengths of the Middle Ages by a dedicated imitation of the great cathedrals of the past, which were symbols of social harmony and art in the service of religious faith. Possibly the Gothic revival was an expression of a rapidly growing industrial society's wish to legitimise itself by seeking its historical roots —rather as the poet Tennyson celebrated the quietly attractive virtues of Victorian bourgeois life in his 1869 epic poem of medieval chivalry, *The Idylls of the King*. Very probably the founders of this Gothic revival style and their patrons were apprehensive that the political and social changes of an increasingly industrialised, urban and democratic society might threaten revolution and the overthrow of a stable social order established during the Middle Ages. If they could copy the outward appearance of an age which they viewed, quite fancifully, as romantic, peaceful and pious, then possibly the modern inhabitants of these 'Gothic' buildings could be influenced to become more godly and conservative.

The physical results of this movement, which was backed by the new wealth of industrial Britain, ranged from the powerful work of original minds (such as those of the architects Pugin and Butterfield) to an ignorant vandalism that demolished or gutted existing buildings not in the fashionable 'Perpendicular' style. The weakness of the movement was that it was based on imitation rather than independent creativity; influential critics such as John Ruskin (1819–1900) and William Morris (1834–96) warned that it was impossible to recapture the spirit of medievalism through the use of industrial techniques and the slavish copying of designs by individual craftsmen who had no say in the final product and no chance of sharing in the buildings that they helped to fashion. The beauty and ugliness produced by this revolution in taste have been the subject of heated discussion in our century, and both sides of the debate are argued forcefully in Kenneth Clark's *The Gothic Revival*, first published in 1928 and then revised heavily in 1962.

Hardy felt, with a certain justice, that the established religion in England in his century was in danger of removing itself from the pressing social concerns of the day. As the events following the death of Jude's children show, the Church at its upper levels had retreated into formal ritual and empty intellectualism, while the great mass of the people were served by over-worked curates like the Mr Highridge who comforts Jude when he is rejected by Christminster. In general, Hardy sees the Church offering no help to his characters in their suffering, and indeed often laying additional burdens on them.

Hardy went to London in 1861 to start his own business, and it was about this time that his hopes of a university career were dashed. He is reticent about the reasons for this, but it seems likely that the authorities found him, like his Jude, under-prepared. The sensitive young man was all too ready to see this as a rejection on the grounds of his social class as well as his education. A career 'combining poetry and the Church' was now out of the question, and Hardy began to write fiction.

While on a small job of church restoration at St Juliot in Cornwall, Hardy met a lady, a Miss Emma Gifford, with whom he fell deeply in love. She sympathised with his literary ambitions but was deeply touched by the social conventions of her day and never forgot that she was born to a higher rank of life than her lover's. Their engagement lasted for four years during which Hardy wrote increasingly successful novels. Their marriage soon became bitterly unhappy and lasted thirty years. It is possible that Hardy's philosophy of disillusion that colours

Jude springs from the disappointment of his private life, but he seems to have been melancholy from his youth and never given to optimism in affairs of the heart. There is some evidence that he had been in love before his marriage with a female cousin who, like Sue Bridehead, was at a Teachers' Training College but we have no real evidence for the strength of their affection. Hardy's disenchanted view of human sexuality and his arguments against marriage in *Jude* are more than expressions of a specific and personal unhappiness. He views sexuality with the detachment of a scientist, as nature's way of providing herself with more lives, unconcerned with questions of affection and morality. Hardy prided himself on being a 'progressive' thinker who believed that once the false glamour and mystery were stripped from the forbidden topic of sex, society would become more tolerant of couples like Sue and Jude. Most people try to bring their personal vision of life to conform with accepted opinions; Hardy believed that an artist was separated from ordinary men by his capacity to see and feel things in an eccentric way which shocked the reader into new insights. He saw his morbid view of the universe as a gift worth cultivating.

Hardy's first novel, which he destroyed, was a satire on the code of class distinction which was going to help to destroy his marriage. It was a false start; Hardy's strengths were to lie in an imaginative rather than a documentary approach to the lives of men and women, and his philosophy was to lead him to discover that social ills were a reflection of the indifference of nature and the laws of survival. His first real success was *Under the Greenwood Tree* (1872), a relatively good-humoured novel about simple country people. After this, Hardy was able to give up architecture completely and launch himself as a professional novelist writing for serial publication in popular magazines. He was a prolific writer and his best-known works include *Far From the Madding Crowd* (1874), *The Return of the Native* (1878), *The Mayor of Casterbridge* (1886), *The Woodlanders* (1887) and *Tess of the D'Urbervilles* (1891). There were frequent problems over his open treatment of sexual emotions and the rougher side of country life, and Hardy often had to compromise with his editors by 'bowdlerising' or refining the text for family reading. Eventually the reading public, which liked undemanding fiction, was appalled by his increasingly dark vision of human life. *Jude the Obscure* (1895) was hailed as 'Jude the Obscene' because of the frank portrayal of its characters' sexual difficulties, the gloom of Hardy's view of the world, and the appalling scene where the children hang themselves. The most intelligent critics praised the novel's power, but it was the last Hardy wrote; possibly he was angered or humiliated by the storm of criticism but more probably he had simply said all that he needed to in the novel form. Jude is the character through whom Hardy most fully expresses man's individual tragic destiny in a society where the old patterns have been broken, and in an uncaring universe.

Hardy turned from fiction to poetry and produced a notable body of work with distinctive tone, coloured like his novels with a bleak pity for deluded hopes, the brevity of individual lives and the disastrous and often comic coincidence that shapes them.

Hardy's curious and very personal philosophy appears to have sprung from his habit of thinking very deeply about his own experiences rather than from those books and ideas that shaped the beliefs of most great Victorians. However he was a painstakingly well-read man and the weight of his bookishness lies heavily on his novels. He is particularly fascinating as a writer since instead of behaving like most authors who take pains to smooth out irregularities of style and eccentricities of imagination in order to produce a world as close as possible to the 'real' one, Hardy insisted on his personal, often unbeautiful prose style, his morbid imagination which dwelt on death, and his vivid bringing of characters to life amid odd perspectives and in natural surroundings charged with symbolic meaning.

A note on the text

Jude the Obscure was first published as a serial in *Harper's New Monthly Magazine* from December 1894 to November 1895. This version was 'bowdlerised' or edited to conform to the cautious taste of a family magazine. It was then published as a book (by Osgood McIlvaine and Company in England and Harper and Brothers in America) in November 1895 with the offending passages restored. The manuscript, by an irony Hardy would have appreciated, came to lie in the Fitzwilliam Museum of the University of Cambridge which had not admitted its author as a student. For modern editions of the text see Part 5, Suggestions for further reading.

Part 2

Summaries
of JUDE THE OBSCURE

A general summary

Jude Fawley, a poor orphan boy, sets his heart on leaving his obscure village for the university city of Christminster. He manages to teach himself the Greek and Latin required for entrance but is trapped into marriage by Arabella, a pig-breeder's daughter. She soon deserts her bookish husband and he works as a stonemason in Christminster where he falls in love with his sensitive cousin, Sue Bridehead. He arranges for her to become assistant to his old schoolmaster Richard Phillotson, but is dismayed when she becomes engaged to the older man. Jude, a mere labourer, is rejected as a student by the colleges. The cousins' strange friendship continues despite Sue's engagement until Jude has to tell her about Arabella. In a fit of pique or jealous anger Sue marries Phillotson and Jude and Arabella are briefly reunited before she runs off to join the man she 'married' after leaving Jude. Sue confesses that she finds marriage physically detestable and Phillotson finally gives his unhappy wife her freedom at the cost of his career. Sue has an incurable aversion to marriage and though she and Jude are soon legally free to marry and she has two children by him, she cannot face another ceremony. Arabella sends Jude the mysterious child of their brief marriage and the Fawley fortunes, never high, decline until Jude has to sell his few remaining possessions and go back to Christminster. His melancholy little son by Arabella learns that Sue is expecting yet another child and hangs himself and her children in a fit of despair. Jude renounces his faith in a loving God, but Sue declares hysterically that the tragedy is a punishment from heaven because she has deserted her lawful husband.

Though still in love with Jude, she returns to be Phillotson's obedient wife. Jude is tricked a second time into marriage with Arabella, and dies in despair while a crowd cheers the Boat Race outside his window.

Detailed summaries

Part First: At Marygreen. Chapter I

Phillotson, the village schoolmaster, quits Marygreen for the university city of Christminster in the hope of becoming a scholar and a clergyman. He leaves his piano with the young night-scholar Jude, and advises him to be kind to animals and birds and to read all he can. Jude is fired with ambition for learning and a hatred of his dull village.

COMMENTARY: Hardy begins by drawing an analogy between Phillotson and Jude, the older and the younger man both sharing the ambition to study at Christminster. He draws a relentlessly unlovely picture of Marygreen, his carefully chosen adjectives emphasising its decay and satirising the modern church in which two loveless marriages will be celebrated.

NOTES AND GLOSSARY:
harlican: (*dialect*) rascal

Chapter II

Jude's aunt, the local baker, tells an aquaintance that Jude is an unwanted orphan and that the Fawley family had better not marry; she speaks of a girl cousin, Sue, who like Jude is 'crazy for books'. Jude is set to keep rooks from a neighbouring farmer's seed-corn and allows the birds to feed off the grain. He is beaten and paid off, to the humiliation of his aunt, and Jude in his disgrace dreams of Christminster as a refuge from the cruelty of the world.

COMMENTARY: Sue is introduced along with the idea of the Fawley curse, and the meanness of Marygreen is stressed further in the conversation in the bakery and the ugly fields where Jude works. The beating that Jude gets points to the central irony or mocking contradiction of our sense of the fitness of things in the novel; those sensitive feelings on which we pride ourselves are a bar to personal survival. Hardy stresses the violence of nature and the hypocrisy of society.

NOTES AND GLOSSARY:
med: (*dialect*) might
tassets: pieces of thigh armour
or'nary: (*dialect*) insignificant, inferior
sprawl: (*dialect*) energy

Chapter III

Jude finds out the direction of Christminster from some workmen, but the city is hidden in mist. He prays to see it and, as if by a miracle, the clouds roll away and he gazes in wonder until night falls. From now on, the idea of Christminster sustains him in his dreary life. He can see the 'halo' cast in the sky by the city lights and he meets a team of carters who give him a garbled account of the classical languages spoken in the university. Jude makes up his mind to go there.

COMMENTARY: After two chapters which have dwelt on the dreariness of the dying hamlet, Hardy emphasises the element of poetry and idealism in the novel as the clouds roll back to disclose Christminster·in her fatal beauty. The charm of the city lies mostly in Jude's imagination and that has its negative side; he has peopled the night landscape with demons. The carters with their commonplace load of coals bring us firmly down to earth.

NOTES AND GLOSSARY:

Herne the Hunter, Apollyon etc.: ghosts and demons from Jude's reading in popular tales of horror and works of devotion

Babel: in the Book of Genesis in the Bible the building of the great Tower of Babel symbolises human intellectual pride which God punishes by the curse of so many different languages. Hardy is commenting obliquely on the vanity of Christminster

Chapter IV

Jude meets the quack-doctor Vilbert who makes his living tricking the local cottagers out of their money. He agrees to provide the boy with books if Jude will publicise his 'cures', but he forgets the promise. Phillotson sends for his piano and Jude encloses a letter asking for grammars of Greek and Latin. After many weeks the books arrive, but Jude finds to his horror that they are incomprehensible without a teacher, and throws himself down in a fit of despondency.

COMMENTARY: Vilbert is a parody of the grown-up Jude in his homelessness and unrecognised claims to learning. The 'road-physician' is the most thoroughly evil character in the novel, preying on helpless men and women and a fit final mate for Arabella. The uncompromising realism and pessimism of this chapter contrast with the poetry of the one before.

NOTES AND GLOSSARY:
quack-doctor: someone who sells worthless cures for sickness
Grimm's Law: a formula by which the Germanic languages of Europe may be shown to have a common origin; a scholarly and difficult version of the 'cipher' or code for which the ignorant Jude is hoping

Chapter V

During the next three years Jude grows to young manhood and manages to teach himself languages by heroic application. He becomes his aunt's assistant and reads as he drives a broken-down horse and van. One evening he finds himself at the scene of his first vision of Christminster and, overcome with pent-up emotion, recites a heartfelt prayer to the moon-goddess. That night he is troubled by his lapse from Christian piety and makes up his mind to study the Bible to fit himself for going to Christminster. He becomes an apprentice stone-mason.

COMMENTARY: Jude's method of study is both heroic and pathetic. Hardy stresses the typically mean jealousy of the villagers who want to stop one of their number from improving himself. The strange evening prayer to the pagan gods suggests the force of Jude's longing for beauty and love which has no natural focus in his narrow life and which will be thrown away on the worthless Arabella in the next chapter. It is ironic that he prays to the goddess of chastity when he is about to be betrayed by lust.

NOTES AND GLOSSARY:
cotter: a labourer who, as part of his wages, was allowed to live in a cottage owned by his employer
sponge: dough set to rise before it is baked into bread
Dido: the tragic queen of Virgil's *Aeneid*, a text studied in great detail by budding classical scholars

Chapter VI

Jude is returning from work, full of grand dreams of his future, when he is interrupted by laughter and a blow on the ear from the pizzle of a slaughtered pig. Three country girls have been struck by his looks and the boldest of them, Arabella Donn, invites Jude to walk out with her that Sunday. Jude is suddenly changed from an austere scholar to a man in search of 'a bit of fun' with the disreputable daughter of a pig-breeder.

COMMENTARY: Hardy shows us what a classical writer would have called the punishment of *hubris* or over-strong self-confidence. This is a frequent device in the novel. Jude is tempted by Arabella's vulgar beauty just as his dreams of the future are most grand. Hardy emphasises the irresistible violence of the sexual passion by the obscenity of Arabella's greeting. The Three Graces of Jude's classical imagination, goddesses symbolising mankind's longing for tranquility and beauty, are parodied by the three girls washing out pig entrails.

NOTES AND GLOSSARY:

the characteristic part of a barrow-pig: Hardy's delicate way of referring to the 'pizzle' or penis of a castrated pig. Arabella throws it at Jude as a very coarse sexual invitation

chitterlings: small intestines that are cleaned and eaten

deedily: strong-mindedly, brazenly

in posse: (*Latin*) potentially

Chapter VII

Jude forgets that he meant to read his Greek New Testament and goes off to the Donn cottage and its pigsties. He takes Arabella to see a distant housefire and they stop at a low inn where he buys beer at her request. She encourages him to kiss her and it is late before they arrive home; Jude is disgusted to find the Donns think of him as Arabella's suitor, but he is overwhelmed by his infatuation. Arabella tells her friends that she must marry this handsome fellow, and they advise her that the usual country way of forcing a man to propose marriage is to conceive a child by him.

COMMENTARY: So strong is the sex instinct that Jude cannot escape his fate. The title-page of the Bible stares at him like 'the unclosed eyes of a dead man', suggesting his own death to come. Hardy uses symbolism to stress the dangers into which Jude is running; the burning house suggests the destruction of his first marriage and the picture of Samson and Delilah shows a woman tempting a man from his principles. Yet Hardy sensitively shows how we feel sympathy for the way the inexperienced Jude idealises this tawdry relationship.

NOTES AND GLOSSARY:

mizzle: (*dialect*) hurry up

Samson and Delilah: the pagan Delilah persuaded her husband Samson to defy God and reveal the secret of his miraculous strength to her; when he did she called in his enemies to blind him and take him into slavery

Chapter VIII

Jude helps Arabella to recapture some escaped pigs. She is vexed by his slowness in courting her and by some neighbours' gossip that he is soon to leave for Christminster. Her parents are sent off to church and she invites Jude in after their usual Sunday walk, embarking on a preposterous flirtation by showing him a hen's egg she is hatching between her breasts and finally leading him upstairs to her bedroom.

COMMENTARY: Jude, like the pigs, is caught, however much he may seek to escape. The episode of the 'caterpillar' in the tree brings to mind the first sin of man in the Garden of Eden and the eternal battle between man's physical and spiritual natures. Arabella's flirtation with the egg looks forward to her assumed pregnancy; she certainly does not want to bring living things into the world and heartlessly abandons the only child she does have. Procreation is only incidental to her appetite for pleasure.

NOTES AND GLOSSARY:

zeed: (*dialect*) saw

gossip: old woman given to chattering about her neighbours

Chapter IX

Three months later Arabella consults Vilbert and that night Jude tells her that they have been acting wrongly and that he means to go away from temptation. She tells him tearfully that she is expecting his child, and he honourably proposes marriage. He is in despair at the ruin of his hopes and by no means in love with Arabella. The villagers are grimly pleased to see his pride humbled. After marriage, Arabella waits for Jude to forget his books and Jude is dismayed to find that Arabella wears false hair and has been a barmaid in a large town. Her pregnancy is a lie, a trick suggested by the wicked doctor.

COMMENTARY: Jude twists in the trap before he is caught. Neither the villagers nor the parson object to a couple expecting a child before marriage; religion is shown to be a matter of superstition rather than morality. We are interested to see how Jude will react when he finds out that Arabella was never pregnant. Though he has no freedom to shape his life—instinct and society see to that—he can choose with what degree of dignity he will face these disasters.

NOTES AND GLOSSARY:

bride-cake: wedding-cake

Chapter X

Jude and Arabella have to kill the pig they have been raising for sale, and when the butcher does not arrive Jude does the slaughtering under his wife's guidance. He spoils the meat by killing the pig too mercifully, and Arabella ridicules his squeamishness. Later Jude overhears Arabella's friends talking about her deceit in marrying him, and when she taunts him with his poverty he tells her quietly that he knows of her lie but will not reproach her.

COMMENTARY: We resent Arabella's matter-of-fact cruelty at the pig-killing, but accept its necessity. The image of blood on the snow tellingly symbolises the battle between the real and the ideal which has shaped the novel so far. We know that the attitudes of Jude and Arabella are completely incompatible.

NOTES AND GLOSSARY:
blackpot: (*dialect*) black-pudding; a country delicacy made with meal and the blood of a slaughtered animal
glane: (*dialect*) sneer

Chapter XI

Arabella provokes Jude beyond endurance, smearing his books with pigfat and abusing him to the passers-by. He realises that his marriage is at an end and goes for sympathy to his aunt, who explains that his family are always unlucky when they wed and that his mother tried to drown herself in an icy pond when her husband deserted her. Jude tries to kill himself the same way but the ice is too thick and he goes off to get drunk. Arabella deserts him for her parents who are planning to go to Australia. She auctions off their few household goods and later Jude finds a photograph of himself, his wedding gift to her, in a dingy second-hand shop window. After he has burned it he feels a free man again. He returns to his resolve to be a better Christian and go to Christminster.

COMMENTARY: Hardy stresses that Jude's disillusionment is not a private burden but part of an inevitable process. As his marriage is ending lovers are passing by on the road outside as Arabella and Jude had a few weeks before; when Jude goes into the broker's shop he finds that other households have been sold up as hastily. The first Part ends on an ironic note; as Jude burns the last relic of his marriage and goes out into the clear night air he believes himself a free man. The seeds of his error with Sue are sown in this self-delusion.

NOTES AND GLOSSARY:
pig-jobbing: pig-dealing

Part Second: At Christminster. Chapter I

Three years later Jude is on his way to Christminster, putting into effect his dream of being a scholar and seeking Phillotson and his cousin Sue Bridehead, for whom he feels a mystical affinity. Jude spends the first night wandering about the ancient streets conversing with the imagined ghosts of dead philosophers until a policeman's question sends him on his way.

COMMENTARY: Hardy stresses the unreal quality of Christminster as Jude perceives it in this feverish and fanciful chapter which is full of ghosts, from the 'haunting' photograph of Sue to the phantoms that throng the streets. Jude himself is to become more and more ghostlike as his attachment to Sue becomes increasingly spiritual and he is stricken with the symbolic disease of tuberculosis or 'consumption' which wastes away his flesh.

NOTES AND GLOSSARY:
Dick Whittington: a beggar-boy who by perseverance and good luck became Lord Mayor of London three times, and married a rich man's daughter; the hero of a folk ballad and obviously the opposite of Jude Fawley

---

Chapter II

In the light of day, Jude finds the colleges less welcoming. He gets work in the yard of a mason who is repairing their crumbling stonework, resumes his study of Greek and cheers himself with the photograph of Sue that he has begged from his aunt. He discovers his cousin at work illuminating texts in a shop and begins to daydream about her. He pretends there is no sexual element in this interest and makes up his mind to introduce himself to her.

COMMENTARY: As usual, Hardy turns from the poetic evocation of a dream to a 'mean bread and cheese question.' Christminster in the morning is 'the defective real' and Jude must find work. It is essential that for a moment Jude should understand the truth, that the intellectual life of Christminster is a sham, and that he should choose, typically, not to act upon this knowledge. Sue is introduced ironically, so that for a moment, like Jude, we believe in her piety and innocence.

NOTES AND GLOSSARY:

Papist ... Evangelical: Hardy is referring to shifts in fashion within the Established Church in the nineteenth century; Aunt Drusilla's generation tended towards extreme Protestantism, while Jude is attracted to something nearer Roman Catholicism

Chapter III

Jude sees Sue in church but the fact of his marriage makes him shy of her. Sue meanwhile is shown to be less religious than Jude thinks her; out walking in the country she has bought two naked statues of pagan gods from an image-seller. She hides these from her pious employer and that night meditates on them in her room at the same time that Jude is intent upon his Greek Testament.

COMMENTARY: Hardy demonstrates the contradictions in Sue's nature in a passage that parallels Jude's prayer to the pagan gods. Her purchase of the naked statues suggests her passionate temperament, yet she immediately covers them, first in the green leaves which identify physical love with nature, and then in brown paper as she becomes desperately afraid of what people will think. Sue will never have the courage to brave out her opinions.

NOTES AND GLOSSARY:

in quo corriget: the Latin version of the text Jude hears

Cyprus: the home of Venus, goddess of physical love. Hardy means that Jude is attracted to Sue because of her beauty rather than her piety

St Mary Magdalen: traditionally, a notorious prostitute turned holy woman, and so in a sense suggesting Sue's later 'conversion' to a narrow religiosity

Julian the Apostate: a Roman emperor who attempted to restore paganism (c.331–63)

Chapter IV

Jude continues to meet Sue unexpectedly and cannot stop thinking about her, though his conscience keeps him from speaking. Sue now seeks him out and they meet; each knows Phillotson, who turns out to be not a clergyman but still a village schoolmaster. He cannot remember Jude but they renew their friendship and Jude is amazed to find how clever Sue is. She has quarrelled with her employer over the statues and Jude asks Phillotson to make her an assistant teacher in his school.

COMMENTARY: Small details symbolise the tragic destiny of the lovers; Sue lifting her skirts to avoid contaminating them with the stone-dust of Jude's trade, and Sue and Jude meeting at the Cross of the Martyr-doms where in former times enemies of society were burned for their beliefs.

NOTES AND GLOSSARY:

erotolepsy: Jude's selfconsciously learned word, meaning seiz-ure by sexual passion

Chapter V

Jude, Sue and Phillotson meet at an exhibition of a model of Jerusalem; Jude is naively entranced, Sue contemptuous of all such Christian devo-tion, and Phillotson alarmed by her attitude. Later Phillotson comforts Sue when she faints during a visit from the school inspector, and Jude, calling on Sue for his Friday visit, finds Phillotson accepted as her lover. Jude, in his 'hopeless, handicapped love,' regrets bitterly that he has brought the two together.

COMMENTARY: Christminster, which the Christian Jude endows with the supernatural glory of the 'Heavenly Jerusalem' or city of God in the Book of Revelation in the Bible, dwindles in Hardy's ironic and worldly view to a scholar's model on a table-top. The reactions of the three main characters to the exhibition neatly sum up their personalities. Jude's journey to the schoolhouse through the rain and his despair at finding that circumstances have driven the weak Sue to accept Phillotson will be repeated in the final Part where the promise of Jude's tragic destiny will be fulfilled.

NOTES AND GLOSSARY:

Calvary: the hill where Christ was crucified. The white cross links it in the reader's mind with the Cross of the Martyrs where Jude and Sue meet

Chapter VI

Jude visits his sick aunt who tells stories of Sue as a child and warns him of the danger of falling in love with his cousin. The villagers' questions about Christminster make Jude decide to seek proper tuition inside a college. Although he is more than half aware that his future lies with the workmen rather than the scholars, Jude applies hopefully to various heads of colleges and receives only one reply, advising him to stick to his trade. In despair at ten years' wasted study, Jude goes out to get drunk, and on his way home writes a bitter quotation from the Book of Job on the walls of the college which had spurned him.

COMMENTARY: Just as Jude seems to have lost Sue her charm is poignantly called up by the village gossips. Their recollections of her, mocking orthodox morality and skating with the boys, show that the adult Sue has kept her childish ways—indeed we see her wading through water again a few chapters on—and that her bravado with men is born of innocence. Hardy has a countryman unknowingly ridicule Jude's faith in Christminster. Symbolically, as Jude decides how pointless his ambition has been, he descends from a high tower to the lowest slums of the city; he turns from idealism to despair instead of to a middle road of sensible conduct.

NOTES AND GLOSSARY:

townish:	(*dialect*) corrupted by the vices of the city
Crusoe:	Robinson Crusoe, in Defoe's novel of that name, tries to escape from the island on which he has been shipwrecked by building a boat which is too large to be dragged to the water.

Chapter VII

Disappointed in all his ambitions, Jude spends the next day getting drunk in a low tavern among labourers, prostitutes and reckless students drinking in a forbidden place. He is invited to prove his learning by reciting the Creed in Latin; when he has, he turns on the rabble in contempt and rushes to Sue's lodgings where he confesses his wickedness in profaning holy things. Sue promises to talk to him in the morning but Jude is overcome with shame and leaves early for Marygreen. His aunt is being visited by a young curate who listens sympathetically to Jude's story and recommends that he enter the church as a clergyman's assistant.

COMMENTARY: Hardy concentrates on the 'other' Christminster which knows nothing of the colleges. The drinkers in the tavern are more of those vagabonds like Vilbert who exist to bring other people down to their level. Jude mistakes the symbolic meaning of his recital of the Creed; it is not the blasphemy he thinks it is, but Hardy uses the episode to provide an ironic demonstration that modern religion is a kind of intoxication that keeps people from using their reason. In his despair, Jude runs like a child to Sue and then to his boyhood home; he still does not want to grow up.

NOTES AND GLOSSARY:

the Creed: a formal statement of Christian belief which is recited as part of the divine service

the Ratcatcher's Daughter: a popular ballad of the nineteenth century

the Laocoön: a famous classical sculpture of a father and his sons being crushed to death by serpents

licentiate: a member of the Church of England who is licensed to preach sermons

---

Part Third: At Melchester. Chapter I

Jude gets a letter from Sue saying that she is at a Teachers' Training College in Melchester. He decides to find employment there while he studies theology, and a second impulsive letter from Sue begs him to come quickly because she is lonely. They have tea together and Jude finds out that she has engaged herself to marry Phillotson. Jude finds work on the repairs to the cathedral and gives himself up to study.

COMMENTARY: In his new piety, Jude makes the ridiculous assumption that a benevolent God has ordained repairs to the cathedral so that Jude can work and study while indulging his attraction towards Sue. The rest of the novel is taken up with showing how Jude learns that no such providence exists and that his decisions are prompted by instinctive urgings. Melchester is like Sue herself, a perplexing mixture of the old and the new; a modern railway station and a dilapidated cathedral, and the modern college housed in an old bishop's palace.

NOTES AND GLOSSARY:

coup de grâce: (*French*) death-blow

tête-à-tête: (*French*) private conversation

harmonium: a small church organ, a musical instrument

Chapter II

Sue and Jude continue to see one another despite her engagement. On a day's outing they miss the train back to Melchester and are forced to spend a night in separate rooms in a shepherd's cottage. The next morning Jude delivers Sue to the College and is rewarded with a small photograph of herself.

COMMENTARY: This is one of the rare moments of happiness the lovers know; they seem to travel back in time to a simpler, purer Golden Age, when men and women lived in harmony and eternal youth, without the need for social institutions. Yet Hardy will not let us enjoy this fantasy uncritically; the shepherd who takes them in is the last of his kind with his cottage falling into ruin, and the holiday ends in mild squabbling and apprehension.

NOTES AND GLOSSARY:

habiliments:	clothing
hurdles:	portable wooden frames made from tree-branches for fences or sheep-pens; these are being covered with tar or pitch to make them more durable
thatch:	a roof made of straw
chainey:	(*dialect*) china
chimmer:	(*dialect*) chamber, room
ba'dy:	(*dialect*) bawdry, indecency
Ishmaelite:	a biblical term meaning 'outcast'; Sue means she is a rebel against society

Chapter III

The College authorities do not believe that Sue's companion is her cousin, and she is punished by being locked up alone. She escapes from her room and wades across the river, arriving dripping wet at Jude's lodgings. Jude makes her exchange her sodden garments for his Sunday suit in which she appears a frail version of himself.

COMMENTARY: The girls in the Training School show how mobile people are in society and how the role of women is changing. Yet Hardy insists on the age-old biological drives which will shape the lives of these girls and make new social customs trivial. Sue's flight across the river, which does not seem a strictly natural action, is powerfully symbolic; she deliberately cuts herself off from her independent girlhood by ruining her reputation and placing herself in a position where she must marry. Her journey is as fateful as that of the human soul in classical literature, making its way across the River Styx which eternally separates the dead from the living. Her putting on of Jude's garments is an emphatic way of showing how closely similar the two characters are.

NOTES AND GLOSSARY:

have it hot:	(*slang*) be severely reprimanded or punished

Chapter IV

Sue is feverish after her wetting and explains to Jude that her attitudes to sex are not conventional. She has a passionate nature but is still a virgin and treats men merely as companions. She explains how in London she had shared rooms with a Christminster graduate who had loved her but who went into a nervous decline and died when she refused to sleep with him. He taught her about books and left her his religious scepticism and a little money which she wasted. Her ridicule of his religion wounds Jude, but he feels that nothing can divide him from Sue.

COMMENTARY: Both Sue and Jude seek forgiveness from each other after their escapades. Sue's character becomes clearer in her feverish confession of her past life. The unfortunate Christminster student is a forerunner of Jude who will die for love of Sue. Her conversation is as always a provoking mixture of borrowed learning, real insights, self-dramatisation and Hardy's own opinions.

NOTES AND GLOSSARY:
brochures: (*French*) loosely bound pages, pamphlets
Ganymedes: Ganymede in classical legend was a beautiful youth chosen to serve Zeus.

Chapter V

The next morning Sue has lost her self-assurance and decides to apply to the College for readmission. Impulsively, she tells Jude first not to love her and then that he may if he wishes. When he next sees her, she explains indignantly that the College authorities have advised her to retrieve her lost reputation by marrying Jude at once; she prettily and unreasonably blames Jude for this humiliation, yet seems pleased that the question of marriage has arisen. Jude cannot bear to disclose Arabella's existence and dwells heavily on Phillotson's claim.

COMMENTARY: Jude and Sue speak at increasingly ironic cross purposes because of the guilty secret of Jude's marriage. This alters the way we look at Sue; if they were free to marry we should suspect her of manoeuvring Jude into a proposal more subtly than Arabella but quite as firmly. However we know that Jude cannot marry her and we pity her belief that she can control events.

NOTES AND GLOSSARY:
dew-bit: (*dialect*) a morsel of food eaten before breakfast

Chapter VI

Phillotson, at the school in Shaston, spends his evenings contemplating Sue's letters and a duplicate of the photograph she has given Jude. Outwardly undemonstrative, he is actually a man of strong passions and finally gives in to his longing to see his fiancee; however when he arrives at the Training School he is brutally informed that she has been expelled for scandalous conduct. He meets Jude at work in the cathedral and is told that Sue is still innocent and that Jude is unable to marry her. That afternoon Jude confesses to Sue that he is married and she is deeply hurt.

COMMENTARY: Phillotson, until now shown as a dull man, is now seen from a new angle as a person of great sensitivity. This complicates our view of Jude's and Sue's relationship; Phillotson is no longer a mere block to Jude's happiness but a character requiring our sympathy and interest. We feel pity for him as he is told so roughly of Sue's disgrace and frantically seeks reassurance from his rival. Jude's long-delayed confession of marriage is dramatically well-handled; the lovers' feelings are repressed because they speak in a public place, but we feel their violence.

NOTES AND GLOSSARY:
Venus Urania: the goddess of heavenly as opposed to physical love

Chapter VII

Sue writes to Jude informing him that she will marry Phillotson within the month, and asks him, as her nearest male relative, to give her away in marriage and arrange for her to lodge under his roof until the ceremony. On the morning of the wedding Sue makes Jude pretend to be the bridegroom and rehearse with her in the cathedral. That afternoon Jude makes her a present of a wedding veil and sees her married to the schoolmaster.

COMMENTARY: Sue's marriage and her behaviour in the weeks leading up to it are distasteful, and her 'rehearsal' of the wedding with Jude is intolerably cruel. Yet we are inclined to share Jude's indulgent view of her because she is so ignorant of the nature of marriage. It is like watching a child about to be punished for some wrong she has innocently done; Sue goes to her doom thinking herself sophisticated but we, like Jude, know better.

NOTES AND GLOSSARY:

to play the Spartan: the inhabitants of Sparta in the ancient world were renowned for their rather uncomfortable physical courage and lack of emotion

a nominal residence of fifteen: the parties to a marriage were supposed to live in the parish for fifteen days before the ceremony could be performed: Sue's ten days' stay with her married cousin is considered evidence of good faith

Chapter VIII

Jude continues to feel 'the oppressive strength of his affection for Sue'. When his old aunt appears likely to die, he writes to Sue, asking her to go with him to take leave of their mutual relative and she agrees to meet him for the journey. Jude gets an offer of a good job in Christminster but he has no heart for the city when he goes back, and tries to drink away his melancholy with Tinker Taylor, a low companion. They enter the tavern in which Jude had recited the Creed and find it fashionably modernised and presided over by Arabella. She is not welcoming but Jude feels obliged to honour their marriage and breaks his appointment with Sue as Arabella becomes his travelling companion. They pass the night at a cheap inn at Aldbrickham as man and wife.

COMMENTARY: Jude begins to realise that no special providence watches over good men and women. Hardy once more uses the imagery of ghosts as Sue slips out of Jude's grasp. The landscape of the novel is altered as Jude becomes more depressed; once familiar places become ugly and 'estranged'. The modern bar suggests the speed with which Jude's world is changing as he concentrates on his inner feelings. Arabella turns up to mock Jude's idealistic adoration of Sue.

Chapter IX

Jude and his wife are not reconciled after their night together and Arabella goes back to Christminster. Jude is horrified to learn that Arabella has married again in Australia and considers the husband of that marriage her 'real' one. As Jude broods on his disgust at having spent the night with Arabella, Sue appears; she had not found him at the station and feared that he was drinking again. Jude keeps Arabella's return a secret, partly for fear of making her criminal second marriage known. Though Sue behaves with great reserve, Jude's aunt predicts that she will 'rue this marrying' and Sue admits that she finds her kindly husband physically repulsive. On his return to Melchester Jude finds a letter from Arabella, explaining that she has gone to London to help her 'husband' to run a public house.

COMMENTARY: Jude's midnight vigil for the spirit of Sue in the previous chapter is mocked by the night he spends in Arabella's bed. The bluntness of his conversation with Arabella is offset in turn by the usual delicate fencing with the unhappy Sue. Hardy has his characters learning from bitter experience and he now makes them go over the ground they travelled in their youth to show how much they have changed and to tighten the bond of shared experience between them.

NOTES AND GLOSSARY:
incarnate: bodiless, spiritual

Chapter X

Jude throws himself into the study of theology and church music. He is strangely moved by a hymn and when he learns that the composer lives not far away, he gives up hard-earned time and money to visit him. The man proves to be shallow and greedy and has given up divine music for the more profitable wine trade. To make matters worse, Sue has written while Jude was on his fool's errand, inviting him to dinner that day.

COMMENTARY: Jude's unworldliness is stressed again; he cannot help believing in people who appear to be godly, and makes the same mistake over the hymn-writer as he did when he saw Sue lettering texts. The merchant shows the way a successful Jude would have sought material success and incidentally how much we should have despised him for it.

Part Fourth: At Shaston. Chapter I

Jude accepts Sue's invitation to visit them in the decaying cathedral city of Shaston. She is sympathetic about his visit to the composer; soon, however, Jude is accusing her of flirtation. In defence, Sue tries to explain how her natural instincts and 'Mrs Richard Phillotson' are at odds. That night Jude watches Sue from the shadows and sees her kiss a photograph.

COMMENTARY: Shaston is a curious blend of the real and ideal, the immoral and the religious. It is as contradictory as Christminster with its colleges and slums. The past weighs heavily upon the self-consciously 'modern' Sue; she teaches in a building which was once a convent and lives in a prison-like ancient house. In this chapter and the next Sue and Jude are physically separated by high window-sills when they speak to and watch one another; a symbol of the way her marriage divides them. The photograph Sue kisses may be that of the dead student; a way of keeping us aware of her destructive effect on men.

Chapter II

Aunt Drusilla dies and Sue arrives in time for the funeral. Sue spends the night at the Widow Edlin's, Jude at his aunt's cottage. They hear a rabbit caught in a trap and meet at Sue's window when Jude goes to put the dying animal out of its misery. In his sympathy for Sue's despair in her marriage, he offers to give up his hope of the church in order to live with and protect her.

COMMENTARY: It is fitting that the new life of the lovers begins at a death; they kiss after the funeral of their aunt as they will kiss and part at the grave of their children. It is an ill-fated love and Hardy stresses his artistic reluctance to let it begin by bringing Sue's train so slowly across the landscape to Jude. The rabbit in the trap symbolises not only Sue and Jude in their respective marriages but their struggle against fate as well.

NOTES AND GLOSSARY:
gin: trap

Chapter III

Sue and Jude kiss passionately when they part. Jude has now cut himself adrift from his former 'respectable' life; he burns his theological books in order to stand as 'an ordinary sinner'. Sue hints at what has happened when she rejoins her husband and that night she does not come to him in bed; he finds her in a cupboard among spiders and rubbish. The next morning she asks permission to go to Jude. It is time to teach their classes, and they communicate all day by means of notes. By that evening Phillotson has agreed to let her have a separate bedroom.

COMMENTARY: This chapter marks the turning point in the novel: the barriers of convention are down between the lovers. Jude burns his books as the Elizabethan playwright Christopher Marlowe's Dr Faustus did, when he was dragged down to damnation; scarcely a lucky beginning for a love-affair. Sue's strange concealment of herself in the cupboard is the instinctive hiding of a bird or animal, not the neurotic action of a spoiled woman. It looks forward bleakly to the discovery of the bodies of her children in another closet; Hardy's novels frequently turn up such grim coincidences.

NOTES AND GLOSSARY:

argumentum ad verecundiam: (*Latin*) to argue by appealing to a higher authority, in this case the nineteenth century political philosopher John Stuart Mill, who believed in the emancipation of women

Chapter IV

Phillotson absent-mindedly enters his wife's bedroom one evening and she flings herself hysterically from the window. The next day he goes for advice to an old school-fellow, Gillingham, who tells him bluffly to smack her and bring her to her senses. Phillotson admits that he respects the idealistic love the cousins have for one another and declares that 'it is wrong to so torture a fellow creature any longer'. He gives Sue her freedom and sends her off to Jude.

COMMENTARY: Sue's leap through the window is a symbolic action of freeing herself after all those conversations over window-sills with Jude. Our pity for the unfortunate Phillotson increases, especially after his visit to Gillingham when he rejects his friend's commonsense advice and follows his humane instinct in letting Sue go. Their parting is a strange blend of the touching and absurd and we are left wholly absorbed in Phillotson's point of view.

NOTES AND GLOSSARY:

newel: the post supporting a stair-rail
toled: (*dialect*) enticed
good-now: (*dialect*) I expect
Laon and Cythna . . . Paul and Virginia: romantic lovers in literature
all abroad: (*dialect*) quite wrong
rafted: (*dialect*) upset, troubled
rummer: large glass

Chapter V

Jude meets Sue, 'a fugitive from her lawful home', on the train, and they travel to Aldbrickham where they will not be recognised. Jude has now left his trade and has agreed to give Arabella a divorce. To his dismay, he learns that Sue will not share a room with him, but she is unreasonably angry when she learns from a chambermaid that Jude has spent a night in the same hotel with Arabella.

COMMENTARY: We begin to sympathise with the apparently successful lover as Sue objects to sleeping with Jude. Her arguments for a woman's right to decide her own sexual conduct may be valid, but they are insincere when they come from Sue, who has a nervous horror of committing herself physically to a relationship. Sue's sexual timidity becomes a metaphor of the terrible loneliness of all the characters in the modern world. Hardy stresses her unreasonable jealousy of Arabella because he is writing to show the complex character of Sue, not the truth of her arguments.

NOTES AND GLOSSARY:
Temperance Hotel: an inn where no alcohol was served, making it a place where a respectable woman could stay without arousing comment

Chapter VI

Phillotson is forced to resign as schoolmaster once his scandalous consent to his wife's elopement is known. He defends himself before a public meeting but is supported only by idlers and vagrants and a riot breaks out. His disappointment makes him seriously ill and Gillingham writes to Sue; she comes to nurse her former husband kindly but her friendship merely torments him. He makes up his mind to give her a divorce.

COMMENTARY: Phillotson's noble action, so painfully undertaken, exposes him to shame and misunderstanding as he is classed with the vagabonds who are ignorantly promiscuous. Sue's return to nurse him is made deliberately unreal; her symbolic turning of the looking glass so that he can see the sun shows how she will allow herself to be admired and loved without involvement, and how she prefers life filtered through poetry and the intellect.

Part Fifth: At Aldbrickham and Elsewhere. Chapter I

By the beginning of the next year Phillotson has divorced Sue and Jude, Arabella. Sue is helping Jude to carve headstones for a living. She fears that her refusal to commit adultery with Jude means that she is not legally free under the terms of the divorce, and she is not enthusiastic about committing herself to a new marriage. The curse of the Fawleys haunts her and she will not love 'by Government stamp' or accept the spurious dignity marriage confers upon a woman. Actually, she is terrified of its physical demands.

COMMENTARY: The fact that both couples are divorced when this Part opens shows that Hardy is pleading for greater tolerance towards informal unions rather than easier divorce. Sue and Jude put on new garments—clothes are highly symbolic of states of mind in *Jude*—and the country through which they walk has been newly seeded for the next year's crop. We feel something is about to happen, as indeed it does in the next chapter. Yet the idea of new beginnings and new growth is offset by the fact that Jude is now a carver of headstones for graves; his love for Sue is still haunted by images of death.

NOTES AND GLOSSARY:

decree nisi: a provisional legal permission to divorce, made final after six months

Chapter II

Arabella calls on Sue and it seems an ill omen. She has been abandoned by her lover and wants to see her former husband. Sue tries to prevent Jude from seeing Arabella but he is firm; neither woman is his wife, through no fault of his own, and Arabella has a claim on his charity. In desperation, Sue agrees to marry Jude and goes to his bed at once for fear of losing him to the 'low-passioned' Arabella. The next morning, much depressed, she goes to see her rival who has just been invited back by Cartlett, her common-law husband. Arabella advises Sue to marry Jude without delay.

COMMENTARY: A crisis has occurred in the lives of the lovers as Sue agrees to sleep with Jude out of a desperate jealousy of Arabella. Hardy suggests that Arabella raises the money to return to London by prostituting herself, which she will do again later to get the money to make Jude drunk. We are invited to compare her open degradation with Sue's denial of her principles when she gives in to Jude. Arabella draws a parallel between the two 'oneyers' or self-willed women.

NOTES AND GLOSSARY:

banns: public notice given in church of intention to marry. By law the banns had to be called on Sunday for three consecutive weeks, to allow anyone objecting to the marriage to speak out

sojer: (*dialect*) a soldier

Chapter III

Arabella's vulgarity makes Sue fear marriage all the more. Sue and Jude read in a newspaper that Arabella has married her publican, and they get a disturbing letter to say that she is sending them Jude's son, a child born during her stay in Australia. Sue feels an immediate pity for the boy who is large-eyed, pale and serious, with a strangely adult air. 'Little Father Time' as the child is called, refers to Sue as 'Mother' and she decides that a legal marriage would help make him happy.

COMMENTARY: Sue and Jude invent the most high-minded and responsible arguments for taking in Arabella's child, but we are more aware of the ironic manipulations of the author as the boy who is about to destroy their happiness sets out with his 'slow mechanical creep' towards their house. Although Sue's fear of the physical side of marriage has been overcome, the forces within and without the lovers that will destroy their relationship are gathering strength.

NOTES AND GLOSSARY:
fly: light one-horse carriage for hire
'bus: horse-drawn omnibus; the cheapest form of transport which carried a number of people at a time

Chapter IV

Jude applies for a marriage licence and the Widow Edlin is invited to the ceremony. She tells more stories about the luckless Fawleys; an ancestor had been hanged as a housebreaker for stealing the body of his dead child from his runaway wife, and the wife ran mad. Little Father Time implores his 'parents' not to marry. The next morning they see a procession of dismal outcasts at the Registry Office and all Sue's aversion comes back. A church wedding seems no wholesomer; to marry at all, she argues, would extinguish their fondness for one another.

COMMENTARY: Widow Edlin's story of the hanged ancestor contains all the elements of the catastrophe about to befall Jude's family; the death of the child, the madness of the wife and the death of the husband. In an unspecified way, Sue and Jude understand that the tale has a special meaning for them. The fog that hovers over this last section of the novel gathers as they make their way to the Registry Office. Their final turning away from the ceremony is psychologically acute; Sue in particular knows that as long as their love is uncertain and unsatisfied it will last, since a romantic passion cannot survive familiarity.

NOTES AND GLOSSARY:

Melpomene:	the Muse or goddess presiding over Tragedy
vitty:	(*dialect*) perfect, exact
gibbeted:	the body of a hanged criminal was exposed on the gallows after execution
incorporeally:	without physical desire
Atreus . . . Jereboam:	doomed families in classical literature and the Bible respectively
sakes if tidden:	(*dialect*) Heaven's sake if it isn't; an exclamation of impatience
game o'dibs:	(*dialect*) children's game played with sheeps' knucklebones

Chapter V

Trains arrive from London and Aldbrickham for the Great Wessex Agricultural Show. One brings Arabella and Cartlett, the other Jude, Sue and Little Time. Arabella is jealous of their pleasure in the child; they seem a happy family whereas her new husband is drinking himself to death. She shrewdly suspects that Sue and Jude are not married. Arabella's old friend Anny laughs at her renewed interest in Jude, and the quack-doctor Vilbert sells her a love potion to be used on her former husband. Sue and Jude, in an ecstasy of quiet happiness, linger over their model of 'Cardinal College, Christminster', and among the flowers.

COMMENTARY: This chapter contrasts with the dismal descriptions of human ugliness in the previous one by dwelling on the exquisite happiness of Sue and Jude, culminating in their complete communion among the roses. Their joy is made to seem all the sweeter by having it spied on by the jealous Arabella and her disreputable friends, who show how Jude's Marygreen past is catching up with him.

NOTES AND GLOSSARY:

excursion-trains:	trains outside the regular time-table, bringing passengers on a day's pleasure-trip

Chapter VI

When Little Time is mocked because his parents are not married, Sue and Jude go off to London where it is assumed that they legalise their union because Sue is pregnant. But the open scandal, so long continued, ruins Jude's trade. He gets a commission to repair the carved lettering of the Ten Commandments in a local church but the parishioners are shocked to see Sue and Jude at work on the holy task and have them turned out of the building. Jude has to resign from a workmen's educational association, bills pour in, and the couple are forced to sell their furniture at an auction while the neighbours gossip about them. Sue's pet pigeons are sold to a butcher and she secretly frees them from their cage, explaining to Little Time that Nature's Law is 'mutual butchery'.

COMMENTARY: The happiness of the day at the Show is now soured by the vindictiveness of the townspeople. Hardy makes Sue and Jude repeat the action of lettering a religious text as Sue had been doing when Jude first saw her; one of those 'mirror-events' in the novel which show how much characters have changed in the interval between. Then Sue and Jude were ignorant of each other's real natures; now they are in perfect understanding. We see a sale of Jude's household for the second time (another mirror-event), and the pleasure we felt in overhearing the private conversation of the lovers at the Show is spoiled now they share our awareness of how many people wish them ill. It is ironic that Sue frees the birds, her special symbols, when in the final part she will refuse to escape from what Gillingham calls the 'cage' of her marriage to Phillotson.

NOTES AND GLOSSARY:

over-restoration:	one of Hardy's jibes at the Gothic revival: churches were often disfigured in an attempt to give them a 'medieval' appearance
Communion-table:	where the Eucharist or most sacred part of the service takes place
voot:	(*dialect*) foot (the Devil traditionally betrays himself by his foot which is shaped like a goat's)
reprobate:	notorious sinner
in my condition:	Sue is now pregnant with her first child

Chapter VII

Jude and Sue labour at casual work for three years, keeping their past a secret. Sue is now the mother of two children and expecting a third. Jude refuses to work on churches and has learned Sue's detestation of Christianity. Arabella and Sue meet again while Sue is selling gingerbread at a fair—Jude, ill and unable to work, has turned to baking again—and Arabella is visiting a local chapel. She has been widowed and has taken up a popular form of religion as a comfort that is 'righter than gin'.

COMMENTARY: Like Sue at the end of the novel, Arabella takes up religion as a consolation in bereavement. Hardy makes the novel's typical association between religious fervour and drunkenness; she has turned from a public-house to a chapel. The cakes Sue sells show how Jude is returning to his Marygreen origins despite his ambition.

NOTES AND GLOSSARY:

chapel: dissenting Protestant Christians worshipped in a *chapel* as opposed to a *church*

ashlaring: giving a stone facade to

standing: a market stall

Chapter VIII

Arabella forgets her newfound religion in lustful thoughts of Jude. She meets Phillotson on her way to Alfredston and introduces herself as Jude's former wife, telling the schoolmaster that his wife's divorce was obtained under false pretences. She advises him that a husband has both the natural and the legal right to force his wife to obedience. Jude tells Sue that he wants to return to Christminster.

COMMENTARY: Arabella's conversion has been laughably brief and her claim that 'feelings are feelings' and must be respected is a parody of the selfless creed of Jude, Sue and Phillotson. Her conversation with the broken Phillotson advances the plot as he now has grounds for taking back his divorced wife. Arabella has learned enough from religion to quote the Bible to prove that a cruel natural law of female submission is backed up by religious authority. Hardy dwells on the unspoiled beauty and peace of the Kennetbridge countryside in order to emphasise Jude's mistake in leaving it for the deceitful charms of Christminster.

NOTES AND GLOSSARY:

chaw high: (*dialect*) to fancy oneself refined or genteel

Part Sixth: At Christminster Again. Chapter I

Sue and Jude arrive in Christminster for the Remembrance Day ceremonies. His old cronies mock Jude, but he defends himself eloquently to the crowd. Phillotson watches the family unseen. When they come to search for lodgings the three children and Sue's obvious pregnancy cause them to be turned away continually. Eventually Sue and her children find rooms but she confesses to an inquisitive landlady that she is not legally married, and is told she must leave. They begin another desperate search.

COMMENTARY: The last Part begins and ends with a day of celebration that mocks Jude's increasing misery. Jude is still under the old enchantment but Little Time sees that the Christminster festivities are like 'Judgement Day'. Jude's 'sermon' to the onlookers is his great public moment in the novel; he shows that he has achieved a greater awareness of life than those giving speeches in the Theatre. Hardy draws an implicit parallel between the Fawley family in search of a place for Sue to bear her child and the Holy Family of Jude's religion; each meets with cold indifference.

NOTES AND GLOSSARY:

Lycaonians: a reference to Acts 14. 5–11 of the Bible. For a brief moment, the crowd admires Jude as the inhabitants of Lycaonia had once wanted to worship St Paul as a god when he preached and performed miracles

jobbing pa'sons: a contemptuous reference to ministers of religion who hire themselves out to preach for money

from Caiaphas to Pilate: from bad to worse. Jesus was transferred from the Jewish court of Caiaphas to the Roman court of Pilate before he was sentenced to death

How do I look now, dear?: Sue tries to arrange her clothing to conceal her pregnant figure

prevarication: telling lies

Chapter II

Little Time catches Sue's mood of fatigue and despair; because people object to children it would have been better if he had not been born. Yet 'mother' has 'sent for' another baby. Sue cannot bring herself to tell him the truth about conception and he continues to blame himself. The next morning she slips out to arrange to take the children to Jude's lodgings and when they return Sue discovers that Little Time has hanged himself and her children in their closet-room and left a note: 'Done because we are too menny'. The children are buried while Sue is prostrate with grief and later Jude finds her hysterically imploring the gravedigger to let her see them once again. When she is taken back to her lodgings she gives birth to a stillborn child.

COMMENTARY: Little Time expresses Hardy's view of the indifference of the universe, but because he is a child he cannot know that affectionate sexuality and intellectual ambition can make the individual life bearable. Hardy piles up the misconceptions and coincidences so that the children ironically die just after room has been found for them. The ironies continue to multiply as an organ plays 'Truly God is loving . . .' and two clergymen argue theology outside the death chamber. Jude's attitude shows what a philosopher he is in his grief; Sue reacts in a purely emotional way. The rapidity of the deaths and burial of the children heightens the drama of the catastrophe; it is like the end of a Greek tragedy where the fall of the hero sweeps his whole family away.

NOTES AND GLOSSARY:

swage: (*dialect*) assuage, lessen

Chapter III

The loss of his children turns Jude against religion; Sue, however, sees the tragedy as a sign from heaven that she must repent and conform. Jude proposes marriage but she declares that she is still Phillotson's wife. Arabella, now keeping house in Christminster for her father, pays a visit of condolence. Sue tells Jude she is convinced that the children have died as a judgement on their guilty love and she refuses to live with him any more.

COMMENTARY: Hardy explains that Sue, like most people, interprets such disasters as the work of a divine power. Only Jude can see that this tragedy springs from a scientific cause. Jude is ironically slow to realise the implications of Sue's unreasonable conversion. Arabella's visit is dramatically necessary; after our emotions have been wrung in the last chapter we need the release of laughter in our appreciation of her hypocritical grief. At the end of the chapter, Jude and Phillotson are exchanging roles.

Chapter IV

Phillotson reads of the tragedy in a newspaper and hears from Arabella that Sue and Jude are no longer living together. Arabella is planning to win Jude back by making Phillotson claim Sue. Desire and self-interest prompt him to do this, since if he marries her he can go back to teaching. He writes asking her to come to Marygreen.

COMMENTARY: Phillotson has turned hypocrite in order to survive in a world which has treated him so cruelly. He decides to win back his sensitive wife by guile, drawing her slowly into the trap of marriage to satisfy his desire for her and improve his social position. It is ironic that Sue, taking her farewell of Jude, should quote 'Charity seeketh not her own . . .' because her obsession with the state of her own soul prevents her from realising that other people deserve her compassion.

Chapter V

Sue behaves like a woman going to her execution rather than her wedding; the night before the ceremony she burns an embroidered nightgown she had worn for Jude. The Widow Edlin warns Phillotson that Sue still loves her cousin, but Phillotson has decided to take a firm line with his wife and will not listen. When they are married he tells her in some pity that he will not force himself upon her.

COMMENTARY: The symbolic fog over Wessex deepens as the characters lose one another. References to death and execution abound to emphasise the horror of Sue's remarriage. The tearing and burning of the nightgown parallel Jude's burning of his books and suggests the violence of the feelings Sue is trying to deny. The marriage in the unlucky new parish church of Marygreen repeats the unholy contract between Arabella and Jude earlier.

NOTES AND GLOSSARY:

open-work:	embroidery
night-rails:	(*dialect*) night-gowns
malice prepense:	a deliberate intention to do wrong
jined:	(*dialect*) joined
junketing:	festivities

Chapter VI

Arabella, temporarily homeless after a quarrel with her father, goes to Jude for help. He takes her in coldly and gives her money to journey to Alfredston for news of Sue. The story of the wedding fills Jude with despair and Arabella with hope; she arranges with her father to trap Jude a second time. Jude is plied with drink until he has to be helped to the Donn pork-shop.

COMMENTARY: Jude now lives chastely with Arabella as he had first done with Sue. Hardy throws the power of the lovers' feelings into relief by having Sue's emotions interpreted through the coarse-minded Arabella. We sense that past events are being picked up and woven together as Jude and Arabella stagger drunkenly past the Martyrs' Cross where Sue and Jude had first spoken, and Jude quotes: 'Though I give my body to be burned, and have not charity, it profiteth me nothing . . .' This refers to Sue's committing herself physically to a love-less marriage.

NOTES AND GLOSSARY:

the varieties of spirituous delectation: a whimsical phrase meaning alcoholic drinks

Chapter VII

Arabella keeps Jude drunk for three days until he is persuaded by the Donn family and their hangers-on that he has compromised Arabella's honour and must marry her.

COMMENTARY: The second betrayal of Jude echoes the first. Time has symbolically stopped in the rooms above the butcher's shop; the lights burn day and night as the revellers gamble and joke. Like Jude, we are confused by the similarity between the two marriages, each of which he has undertaken to save Arabella's non-existent honour. The fortunes of Sue and Jude are keeping parallel even though they are apart; each is degradingly married.

NOTES AND GLOSSARY:

flitch: side of bacon
Capharnaum: Jude recalls that the biblical Capharnaum was a town where sinners dwelt in wilful ignorance of salvation
the W---- of Babylon: a biblical reference. The Whore of Babylon in the Book of Revelation is the symbol of the lusts and luxury of the world, and as such, aptly applied to Arabella
hyperbole: overstatement for dramatic effect
'prentice: apprentice

Chapter VIII

Jude marries Arabella and they quarrel continuously. He wants to see Sue but Arabella insults her rival and Jude attacks her in a fury. She writes a letter of invitation but does not post it, and Jude goes through the pouring rain to Marygreen, where he meets Sue in the church. She will not return to him because of her new beliefs, but she admits that she does not sleep with her husband. Jude leaves her for the last time.

COMMENTARY: Hardy satirises marriage bitterly. Jude is more ghostlike than ever as he journeys through the driving rain and he and Sue are like spirits as they say farewell to each other in the church. After they have parted he flings himself down by the milestone near the gibbet or gallows which had held the body of his ancestor, and seems to be sinking down into the obscurity of the grave.

Chapter IX

Jude tells Arabella that he has visited Sue in order to kill himself. He seems to see the spirits of the dead laughing at him in the streets of Christminster. Sue confesses to the Widow Edlin that she still loves Jude and that to mortify this weakness of the flesh she will offer herself as a wife to Phillotson. She goes to his room and swears to obey him.

COMMENTARY: Jude becomes less and less of a physical being as Sue finds out too late that she loves Jude 'grossly' or physically, and is trapped by her mistaken religious principles into making a grotesque sacrifice of her body to Phillotson.

NOTES AND GLOSSARY:
sperrit:	(*dialect*) spirit, ghost
un-ray:	(*dialect*) undress
jumps:	under-bodice

Chapter X

Jude lives on until the summer. The Widow Edlin tells him of Sue's new relations with her husband. Jude turns the quack-doctor Vilbert out of his house but Arabella has her eye on a third husband and offers Vilbert his own love-potion.

COMMENTARY: Hardy does not let Jude die in happy ignorance of Sue's sacrifice. His mental agony is mocked by Vilbert's coarsely comic and lecherous courting of the widow-to-be downstairs.

Chapter XI

Jude lies dying while Arabella dresses herself in her finery. She slips out of the house and Jude repeats Job's lamentations in the Bible, his last words ironically punctuated by the cheers of the Boat Race crowd. Arabella returns briefly to find him dead, but she is unwilling to lose her fun and goes down to her friends again. She flirts with Vilbert while her husband 'sleeps' and when she does go home, calls in on the way to demand the services of a corpse-washer and sexton. Two days later Arabella and the Widow Edlin stand over Jude's open coffin talking of Sue, who will not come to the funeral. She says she has found peace, but neither woman believes it.

COMMENTARY: Christminster's holiday spirit is echoed in Arabella's flightiness as she dresses to go out and desert her dying husband. Jude's intelligent despair expresses itself in the great prose of the Book of Job, and Hardy ironically shifts our attention between the dying man and the frivolous woman. We do not see Jude die, because he has already died in spirit by the milestone outside Marygreen where he had carved his hopes of Christminster. Today he has spoken his own epitaph and Hardy has allowed him, with great tact, to slip away 'off-stage'. Arabella's imperceptive remark that he is 'a 'andsome corpse' hardly touches him.

NOTES AND GLOSSARY:

sexton: a church officer who rings the bell to mark a death and who digs graves

Honorary degrees: degrees not based on academic ability but awarded in this case to members of the nobility who bring money and notoriety to the university. Recently such degrees are awarded to honour outstanding achievement in various areas of life, academic and other

gents: (*vulgar*) gentlemen

Part 3

Commentary

The achievement of *Jude the Obscure*

A general approach to the novel

Like all great literary works, this novel is about many things: character, fate, and the way in which people manage to endure their lives by creating ideals by which to live. The characters in *Jude* live by many different values. Arabella, for example, believes in mere survival. Sue insists on living her life according to a succession of contradictory beliefs: she places her trust in her intellect at first, and after losing her children prostrates herself before a vengeful God in whom Hardy does not believe. Jude worships first Christminster and then Sue. Hardy seems to be saying that though one may write a novel showing that the world we live in is indifferent to us as individuals, we cannot actually live in such a vacuum of faith; we must create a context for our lives even if it is a false and vicious one, such as Sue's return to a loveless Christianity.

Jude the Obscure takes as its hero a remarkably ordinary young man. He is able to merge almost invisibly into the crowds of workmen, and to the students of Christminster Jude is merely

> a young workman in a white blouse, and with stone-dust in the creases of his clothes; and in passing him they did not even see him, or hear him, rather saw through him as through a pane of glass at their familiars beyond. (2.II)

Yet in his ordinariness Jude is Hardy's final example of how we all struggle to make some sense of the world. Jude and Hardy begin with very different standpoints: Jude is at first a committed if naive Christian, hoping for a life in the Church and trying to understand the wrong turns his life takes as messages from his God. Hardy was unable, like a good many scientifically-inclined men of his time, to believe that a God intervenes in human affairs. He saw the miseries and disappointments of this world not as a process for testing the human soul, but as the outcome of Nature's careless use of sensitive men and women in the blind generation of new lives.

People often view *Jude* as a work of ultimate pessimism and Hardy as despairing of the human condition. But Hardy probably saw himself as a scientific observer of what happens when Jude's nineteenth century optimism—he believes in self-improvement, God's providence and progress by will-power—tries to impose itself on the indifferent world of Nature and vindictiveness of human social institutions. Hardy uses his role as the *omniscient narrator* or all-knowing story-teller to detach himself from Jude and show his hero as the dupe of his own good nature.

> . . . He was a boy who could not himself bear to hurt anything. . . . This weakness of character, as it may be called, suggested that he was the sort of man who was born to ache a good deal before the fall of the curtain upon his unnecessary life should signify that all was well with him again. (1.II)

The world does not value kindness. The survivors who live to comment on Jude's death have learned to do without it. 'Poor folks must live', cries Arabella contemptuously. 'What's God got to do with such a messy job as pig-killing, I should like to know.' 'Cruelty is the law pervading all nature and society; and we can't get out of it if we would!' says the schoolmaster Phillotson with 'biting sadness' after he has suffered for letting Sue go to her lover. Every time Jude tries to act by the principle of kindness he is led further to his eventual defeat. He is thrashed for letting the birds eat the surplus seedcorn, he is married to Arabella because he cannot bear her humiliation, and he is led on to his second and more fatal love affair because Sue writes to him that she is lonely. Sue attempts to impose her own sense of refinement on the world by intellectual effort; she sees things not as they are but as she would like them to be, and the shock of losing her children unhinges her reason.

Hardy views all this as a personal tragedy for the lovers but for most of the action he dissociates himself from their interpretation of events. We cannot doubt the extent of the parents' grief as they stand by the newmade grave of their children, but part of Hardy keeps aloof from their misery. If they had expected less from life, if they had not trusted other people, if they had respected the power of social institutions, they would have survived. Their idealism destroys them. The survivors in the novel are pirates like Arabella and her third husband Vilbert who prey knowingly on the vices of other people, or unheroic men like Phillotson who know when they are beaten and end up as what Hardy saw as average cruel members of society. We admire Sue and Jude, but we understand that their tragedy is inevitable in a world ruled by 'the survival of the fittest'.

Jude as a nineteenth century hero

Hardy's last novel comments on the nature and values of the novel during the nineteenth century. Jude is the latest in a long line of heroes who are of relatively lowly birth but possess more than their share of poetry and ambition: Dickens gave us David Copperfield, Thackeray Barry Lyndon and Trollope Phineas Finn. All these young men become socially acceptable and even quietly famous, despite unfortunate episodes with women; the woman either dies or jilts them. They take on the values of a worldly society, cease to make fools of themselves and seek money and position instead.

Hardy takes this very common theme of a young man's education and asks what would happen if the young man believed that he was right and the world wrong. Arabella does not have the tact to die, but keeps reappearing at the most inconvenient moments, even when safely divorced. Jude keeps interpreting his untrustworthy fellow men in the light of his own transparent kindliness; nor will he give up his old love, Christminster. In many ways Jude is more attractive than the sophisticated heroes of other novels who pack their capacity for moral outrage away with their boy's clothing, but it is an impractical decency. The greedy composer who gives up church music for the wine trade shows the way a successful Jude would have gone. 'It would have been better for him in every way if he had never come within sight and sound of the delusive precincts, had gone to some busy commercial town with the sole object of making money by his wits, and thence surveyed his plan in true perspective', Jude decides of himself in a rare moment of clear-headedness. (2.VI) Phillotson manages to arrange tidy compromises between his personal and social values; Jude, with his contempt for hypocrisy, decides to live openly as a sinner. Jude is a reproach to most prudent human conduct, and Hardy takes plenty of opportunities to draw comparisons between his stonemason hero and the founder of Jude's religion who was destroyed when he tried to make people live by an ideal moral code.

Technological change and the world of the novel

If Hardy's Jude takes his place in this timeless tragedy of human characters in conflict with the demands of social institutions, he is also an individual. His strongest feelings and ambitions have been formed specifically by the new inventions of his century. We notice that the characters in the novel are shifted about by the railway train; as Sue aptly says, the railway station has replaced the cathedral as the focus of modern life. People travel and cannot be kept in ignorance of the world and new ideas. Jude, Phillotson and Sue follow their trades in one place or another as work offers or scandal drives; cities give Sue and Arabella their very different sexual educations. Sue's freedom to travel has detached her from her relatives, given her a profession and emancipated her mentally. The Donns and Father Time return from the other side of the world. Freedom to travel and the possibility of change, symbolised by the intersecting railway lines and the cheap day excursion, broaden the mind and awaken ambition. But there is a darker side to all this; all the characters in the novel are adrift, cut off from their roots. There is a dreadful sense of individual isolation, reinforced in many stylistic and thematic ways. The characters wander through a series of bleak lodgings carrying only the most minimal possessions—a photograph, a bag of tools, a few books, a family sofa—bare reminders of a past that is lost but which is eloquently called up in the values and conversation of the Widow Edlin. It is no accident that the most poignant moments in *Jude* occur when the characters express the deepest emotion in public or impersonal surroundings: Jude confessing his first marriage to Sue amid the untenanted and refuse-laden stalls of the deserted market, their brief moments of perfect happiness in the crowd at the Agricultural Show, Sue giving birth to a dead child in the house of a grudging landlady, and Jude dying alone in lodgings while an indifferent crowd cheers the Boat Race outside his window.

A second modern invention which directs the course of the plot is the photograph. Jude and Phillotson both cherish duplicates of the same portrait, a handy symbol of how Sue divides herself between the two men while keeping the 'negative', her physical integrity, in her own possession. A photographic likeness passes into relative immortality and so emphasises the frailty of the flesh and the continuity of memory; Sue keeps a photograph of her dead London lover by her bed. When Arabella flings away her husband's likeness it is a desecration; when he burns it, we feel that in some way he will bring about his own death. Hardy never uses the inventions of his lifetime idly, but makes us aware of the unalterable change these things have made to the way we see ourselves.

Hardy's Wessex

Hardy took his own county of Dorset, expanded it into some of the outlying territory, and created his famous 'Wessex', a fictional landscape of unusual vividness. The geography of *Jude* is poetic in its symbolism, the different towns and villages representing stages in the world's evolution out of a dying medievalism. What makes 'Wessex' so powerful a force in *Jude* is Hardy's insistence on the weight of past history. In their daily lives Sue and Jude cross roads once highways but now no longer used; the Roman way outside Marygreen is now only a footpath, and the Land's End highroad is bypassed by the Great Western Railway. Hardy's grand view of human history sweeps the individual life into poignant oblivion.

Hardy as a thinker

It must be said that Hardy was not really an original thinker, even though later in his life he came to believe that he was. His value lies in his ability to gather up and extract poetry from ideas that had already been current for half a century: religious doubt, female emancipation, investigation of mental abnormalities, and the theory of natural selection put forward by Charles Darwin in 1859 which led certain individuals to challenge the idea of a benevolent Creator. Hardy was concerned not so much with the ideas themselves but with the impact that they made on his own eccentric world-view. Hardy may have been writing at the same time as writers such as Ibsen (1828–1906), Strindberg (1849–1912) and Shaw (1856–1950) who attacked social injustice, but he is working towards a different end. He prided himself on his liberal opinions and sees himself in *Jude* following in the footsteps of that great poet, moralist and enemy of the Established Church, John Milton (1608–74). Hardy has excellent intellectual and personal reasons for arguing against the idea of indissoluble marriage, and for people's right to free unions based on love, though we must remember that Hardy took care to present himself to the world as a most respectable man and a loyal husband. But we cannot really accept *Jude the Obscure* as a serious argument against the convention of marriage; Sue and Jude are a most abnormal couple. Sue's trenchant, witty sallies against wedlock become pathetic when we realise that she herself detests physical passion. Jude's tolerance of her frantic distaste for sexual love is, as he admits, unusually kind. They can hardly be taken as spokesmen for normal members of society and their problem is not a common one. What is deplorable is the cruel vengeance society takes on this harmless couple. Victorian readers were offended by the slurs the characters cast on married love, that most sacred of unions, and few readers today probably feel quite comfortable with the 'bodiless' comradeship of the cousins and turn with some relief to the earthiness of Arabella. Hardy is sensitively aware that Jude's and Sue's love remains undiminished because it is unsatisfied; theories of 'Platonic'—or non-physical—love have always suggested that the partners perceive love as ennobling, that one searches for one's mirror-image among members of the opposite sex, and that love, to remain perfect, must not be physically expressed. All this holds true for the cousins, where Sue is Jude in female dress and he worships her mind and spirit.

Hardy's metaphysic

Hardy makes it plain that he finds the religion of Victorian England inadequate to care for and explain the human predicament. As Sue and Jude agonise over their dead children, two clergymen outside quarrel over a minute point in the church service; the church at Marygreen has been paid for by hypocrites like Troutham and the old church, a link with the village past, torn up and abused by greedy men. There is no sense in Hardy's novels of a hand other than the author's guiding the action and manipulating the fates of the characters. Jude readily interprets simple sexual feeling or natural self-interest for divine messages, but Hardy dismisses this as 'superstition' on his part; Jude has to unlearn his naive belief in a special providence that watches over him before he can acquire the self-knowledge of a tragic hero. The more intellectual Sue has reasoned that her whole life has been 'shaped' by her sexual frigidity, and Hardy approves of her understanding. Jude is referred to at one point as 'predestinate', not because God has the outcome of Jude's life already in hand, but that, given Jude's habits of kindness and reflectiveness, society is going to make short work of his happiness. The idea of character as destiny probably goes back to the classical authors Hardy and Jude read. In addition, Aunt Drusilla introduces the idea of heredity as a kind of destiny; when she claims that Fawleys should not marry for fear of inheriting the family curse it sounds melodramatic, but Hardy is instinctively anticipating the discoveries of modern genetics. The Fawleys certainly do inherit a morbid temperament. A belief, however vague, in the power of physical and moral qualities to reappear in later generations is a belief in fate of a sort.

Hardy believes that the universe is not hostile to man, merely indifferent to him. It is therefore surprising that things go against the expectations of the characters so often; in a universe governed by blind chance one would expect a fair amount of good luck as well as bad. The constant downward slide of Jude appears to suggest a purposeful malevolence or ill-wishing of the character by an intelligent Power. Hardy would say that his intention is to make us aware by a little artistic emphasis that we cannot count on any special treatment just because we are precious in our own sight; he uses the artist's privilege and emphasises the ruthlessness of his characters' destruction to show that there is no spirit of fairness or compassion at work in the universe.

Style and structure in *Jude the Obscure*

Plot

If we think of *Jude the Obscure* as the story of a young man of humble birth who wants to go to university, we are bound to wonder why Hardy abandons this idea so early. By the end of the Second Part it is clear that Christminster has rejected Jude except as a lowly workman repairing its stonework, and though Jude cherishes his pathetic hopes until his last return to the city, Hardy shows brutally how pointless they are. The story of Jude and his ambition to be a scholar is in fact a *sub-plot* or *prologue* to the main interest of the novel: the strange account of Jude's love for his cousin Sue, its partial fulfilment and his eventual loss of her. Jude's passion for Christminster foreshadows his more intense infatuation with Sue. We can see the twin plots involving Christminster and Sue as aspects of Jude's constant search for the ideal. In the dismal village of Marygreen it is easy to believe that Christminster is 'the heavenly Jerusalem', even when Jerusalem is reduced, in the world of the novel, to a shoddy replica on a tabletop, and Christminster is actually 'four centuries of gloom, bigotry and decay'. Jude even more foolishly worships the capricious and unstable Sue, believing that she embodies all that is best in his own nature, until she betrays him unwillingly at the end. *Jude* is not about the rights of the working man to attend university, since Hardy has Jude say twice in the novel that these rights have been won by men younger than himself. The theme of *Jude* is the inevitability of Jude's defeat, given the forces at war in his personality and his worship of false gods.

In an important aspect the plot of Jude is *linear*; that is, it begins with the boyhood of Jude and continues in an orderly fashion until his death, dwelling on the most significant events of his adult life. Hardy selects those incidents which form a *pattern*; instances of Jude's tenderheartedness, his vulnerability to women, and his readiness to pursue ideals. Therefore the plot of *Jude* is made up of *repeated events*: Jude and his son are both abandoned by a heartless parent, Jude like his mother attempts suicide by drowning, Arabella twice forces Jude to marry her, Sue and Jude go to one another in their disgrace, Sue hides from her husband in a cupboard, and it is in a cupboard that she finds her children dead. These episodes are more than coincidence; they show that the characters know that they are in the power of the past, of heredity, or traits in character that cannot be rooted out. The plot of *Jude* is carefully *balanced* in the manner of an hourglass, in that Sue and Jude exchange their intellectual positions in the course of the action. Jude begins as a devout if rather naive Christian, and dies cursing an unmoved God; Sue begins as a fashionable agnostic, and ends devoting herself to an imaginary God of Wrath whom she believes has destroyed her children to bring her to repentance. Sue's retreat into fanaticism shows her pathetic vanity and her refusal to admit that she cannot control her life; Jude, on the other hand, has been 'educated' by his terrible sufferings and has emerged with a stronger sense of his own identity. Finally, the plot of *Jude* is based on *contrast*, with the pairs too long to list: Sue and her heathen gods, Jude and his Greek Testament, Jude the theological student and Jude the adulterer, the earthy Arabella and the saintly Sue, the colleges and slums of Christminster . . . and so on.

Language

Perhaps it helps us to read this long and elaborate novel if we recognise that Hardy's prose style is difficult; dense, clotted with quotations and sometimes halting in sense. We may feel that Hardy's strength lies in the acuteness of his visual imagination—he manages to suggest all the tragic bravado of Sue in the way she cocks her thumb up the handle of her sunshade—and the sad irony of his superimposed descriptions of altered states of mind; the landscape around the Brown House becomes charged with different meanings depending on who is observing it during the courtship and marriage of Jude and Arabella.

Dialogue in *Jude* is a particularly thorny problem. The private thoughts and feelings of the characters are described with greater sensitivity than their conversations. Sue and Jude address each other as if at a public meeting, even in their most intimate exchanges, and their lovers' conversations would be more appropriate in the lecture room. They court each other by exchanging information. This could be because their knowledge is so hard-won that the sharing of it is a gift; at all events, the stilted words of the cousins emphasise the fragility of their bond and their essential loneliness. The dialogue of moral opposites is a worse problem; Sue and Arabella and Arabella and Phillotson speak together on several occasions and these tend to be stagey and awkward moments. However interesting the material talked about (these are times when the plot is urged forward) we have a 'dialogue of the deaf' with no real communication going on.

There are exceptions to this general rule of stilted conversation.

Phillotson redeems himself by his visit to his old friend Gillingham, where they both lapse back into the comfortable dialect of their boyhood days. Hardy uses language to demonstrate how Phillotson has been robbed of his spontaneity by his professional training, and how he had the potential of a Jude until it was wrung out of him by rules of schoolmasterly behaviour. His unpretentious and direct speech prepares us for his uncharacteristic decision to follow his instinct and let Sue go to her lover. Finally, there are times when a halting conversation conveys an unbearable poignancy to the reader. Sue answers Little Time's questions about conception abstractedly, her mind on the birth of her child and the difficulty of getting lodgings; in his belief that he is responsible for the family's plight the boy kills himself and the children.

There are isolated splendid speeches in *Jude*; almost romantic lyrics. The aunt and her village gossips talk of Sue as a girl:

> She was not exactly a tomboy, you know; but she could do things that only boys do, as a rule. I've seen her hit in and steer down the long slide on yonder pond, with her little curls blowing, one of a file of twenty moving along the sky like shapes painted on glass, and up the back slide without stopping. All boys except herself; and then they'd cheer her, and then she'd say, "Don't be saucy, boys," and suddenly run indoors. They'd try to coax her out again. But 'a wouldn't come. (2.VI)

The image of the children 'like shapes painted on glass' is perfectly in keeping with the old woman's limited stock of experience and also conveys the fragility of Sue's moral and emotional balance as an adult. Hardy usually writes best when he writes dialogue for country folk and least well when he attempts the tones of the gentry. On the same page as the fine description of Sue we find that Jude's painfully sincere but secondhand quotations in praise of Christminster are skilfully overset by a neighbour's contempt for the city's irrelevance to his own experience:

> As I say, I didn't see nothing of it the hour or two I was there; so I went in and had a pot of beer, and a penny loaf, and a ha'porth of cheese, and waited till it was time to come along home.

Hardy may have learnt the value of such compensatory earthiness from Shakespeare, who let shrewd simple men set their betters right (Widow Edlin is like the Nurse in *Romeo and Juliet*), but it is more likely that he remembered the authentic voices of his own childhood.

The failure of much of the dialogue in *Jude the Obscure* to suggest real communication ends by having a positive effect. Hardy emphasises the value of feelings that lie beyond verbal expression, and in particular the mystical attachment of the cousins. We see why he plays down mere spoken words when he describes with such immediacy the lonely grief of Jude.

Another trait of style in this novel is frequency of quotation; not just Jude's habit of filling his conversation and private thoughts with references to his reading, but Hardy's own insistence on his learning as an author. This can often be irritating, but it has a useful deeper meaning. It can be Hardy's way of suggesting a community of feeling between the present and the past; all that the characters suffer in the present has been endured by others. On at least three occasions Jude expresses the fulness of his joy or misery by quotation: his prayer to Diana and Apollo, which releases all the useless power of imagination and love that has been pent up in him, the verse from the Book of Job which he writes in chalk on the college gates ('I have understanding as well as you; I am not inferior to you, yea, who knoweth not such things as these?'), and his borrowing from the *Agamemnon*, a tragedy by the Greek dramatist Aeschylus (525–456 BC) which shows that Jude has achieved self-mastery: 'Things are as they are, and will be brought to their destined issue.' Quotation is the only way an uncreative man can rise to poetic utterance, and Hardy makes touching use of Jude's borrowings from other men's intellectual riches.

Point of view

Like most nineteenth-century novelists, Hardy believed that the author was supposed to know the past, present and future of his characters and that he had the right to interpret their unseen actions and pass judgement on them in the text. This convention of the *omniscient* (*all-knowing*) *narrator* is indispensible to Hardy's *ironic* view of his characters' destinies and the malignity of chance. We are allowed to see characters engaged in activities at odds with their social roles: Jude the religious baker worshipping pagan gods in the moonlight, the pious and virginal Sue reverencing naked statues, the unbending Phillotson kissing the portrait of his fiancee. Hardy's revelations of the hidden aspects of people stress the richness of feeling and complexity of motive that social conventions ignore in the individual. If we had seen Sue only in terms of her outward actions, for example, we should judge her as Gillingham does: a trivial flirt.

Hardy can play the part of destiny in arranging his characters' lives. He has Jude cut down by Arabella's coarse missile just as he is imagining a blasphemously grand future for himself. Jude's childish vision of

Farmer Troutham's field as a workplace for himself and a granary for the birds is supplemented by Hardy's intelligent pessimism:

> Every inch of ground had been the site, first or last, of energy, gaiety, horse-play, bickering, weariness. Groups of gleaners had squatted in the sun on every square yard. Love-matches that had populated the adjoining hamlet had been made up there between reaping and carrying. Under the hedge which divided the field from a distant plantation girls had given themselves to lovers who would not turn their heads to look at them by the next harvest; and in the ancient cornfield many a man had made love-promises to a woman at whose voice he had trembled by the next seed-time after fulfilling them in the church adjoining. (1.II)

Jude instinctively hopes that his future will be brighter than his fellow-villagers', because it is human to believe that a special fate awaits one. Hardy takes no such interested view, and shows that disillusionment is as much a part of the natural cycle as seed-time and harvest. Later, when Jude has been disappointed by the Greek and Latin books which he cannot read, he flings himself down and is 'an utterly miserable boy for the space of a quarter of an hour'. Hardy makes us aware that the adult Jude will know misery the child cannot guess at; when Hardy offers us the chance of some adult coming to dispel Jude's worries, he snatches it away with 'But nobody did come, because nobody ever does.' The universe is indifferent, and here the author mimics that cruel carelessness. Hardy believes only in the laws of chance and the scientific theory of the survival of the fittest, and ironically mocks those characters who search for a pattern in the universe.

Character development

We notice very quickly that all the characters represent some aspect of Jude himself, without giving up their individual vitality. Jude himself is both a symbolic hero and a real man; he has echoes of the founder of the Christian religion (he is a workman and a teacher, preaches to the multitude and is a sacrifice to his principles of charity), heroes of tragic drama and of the Bible (Job, tried by his God, and Samson, betrayed by the love of women.) Sue is Jude's blood relation and represents his own best opinion of himself; at one point she wears his Sunday clothes to intensify this point. He is so enchanted by her charm, sensitivity and cleverness that he cannot see that her qualities are dangerously double-edged, and we see his fate foreshadowed in the story of the student killed by this cruelly chaste young woman. Arabella represents the links Jude still has to his Marygreen heritage; he aspires to Christminster and she to a London gin-palace, but each is an ambition in its way. In her shameless earthiness she parodies those physical desires which humble him in his pursuit of godliness and Sue. Sue and Arabella may strike us as a modern version of that Sacred and Profane Love which was a favourite theme of Renaissance artists; two women of equal but different beauty are shown competing for the attention of the observer, one symbolising his spiritual nature and the other luring him through physical desire to earthly concerns. A modern novelist might well prefer a sexually competent woman like Arabella, but Hardy sees through Arabella's sexual frankness to a dangerously artificial element in her nature; he prefers the sensitive Sue. Phillotson, too, echoes Jude's history in a minor key; he too is Sue's husband, he cherishes hopes of entering Christminster, and he is rejected by society when he tries to act according to his conscience. Ironically, this mirror-image of Jude is forced to be his rival.

Other characters act as *choruses* to the tragedy. Aunt Drusilla offers melodramatic warnings, the Widow Edlin acts as comic relief, unable to understand the delicacy of conscience that prevents two people in love from marrying, and the enigmatic Gillingham offers a Plain Man's Guide to the strange actions of the figures in the central triangle. Physician Vilbert circles the action like a malevolent planet, always on hand with evil advice and a parody of Jude in his parade of learning. Tinker Taylor and Mr Donn show the impossibility of Jude's ever sinking back into the class from which he has freed himself by thinking and reading. Jude is seen throughout as viewed in a multiple mirror, first this side and then that of his personality emphasised, caricatured or softened, while the characters who illustrate Jude's traits remain sturdily independent and a gathering of social types from Victorian England.

Symbolism, metaphor and imagery

The physical landscape in which the characters move has the independent force of an unseen personality shaping their lives and commenting on their actions. Christminster, that focus of Jude's emotions, is almost his first mistress; his unrequited love can easily be channelled towards the available Arabella. On his first visit to the city Jude is enchanted by its glamour and the ghosts with which his imagination peoples it; the next morning the magic has vanished and the stonework is rotten and decayed. The last time Jude returns to his beloved city, Christminster is a grim collection of blackened walls, grim gaol-like colleges, slums and cemeteries; as he lies dying Arabella merely echoes the flighty indifference of the celebrating city. Marygreen, Jude's adopted home, is a relic of an earlier time like Aunt Drusilla; decayed and played-out, spoiled by 'townish' additions. Shaston is a reflection of Phillotson's obsession with the dead past and prudent behaviour, so that wherever Sue turns in her new home she finds the limitations of her marriage magnified. Melchester possesses both a cathedral and a railway station; as cross-roads of the old world and the new it is a fitting place for Sue and Jude to choose their courses in marriage or the church.

When Sue and Jude are happiest they are free wanderers in Wessex owing allegiance to the values of no particular place. Their loveliest moments together are first at the shepherd's hut near Wardour Castle and later at the Agricultural Show. In the first instance, the cousins escape to a brief idyll 'outside all laws except gravitation and germin-ation' on a half-holiday for Sue, and become briefly a shepherdess and her swain from an imaginary age of innocence, Sue with the symbolic shepherd's crook that Jude makes for her. But the modern world has caught up with them even here; the shepherd they meet knows about railway timetables and cannot find a thatcher for his picturesque cottage. Old country ways are a luxury the changing world cannot afford. Where you live in *Jude the Obscure* determines what happens to you, and when Jude casts in his lot with Christminster, he is lost.

The animal imagery with which the novel is filled suggests the pain caused to the individual by institutions designed by man to keep his fellows in order. Phillotson tells Jude in the opening chapter to be kind to animals and Jude takes him at his word; he is already too kind to step on the writhing, copulating earthworms, a symbol of sexuality at its blindest and most degraded. The killing of the pig, Jude's poor 'fellow-mortal' and symbol of his sexual nature, shows how Jude has been victimised at the hands of that Lady Macbeth, Arabella. In this life it is necessary to maintain your own existence by killing another being for food. The birds which Jude is beaten for feeding appear and reappear in the novel, almost always associated with Sue Bridehead, and when at last she releases her pet pigeons from the butcher's cage we have an ironic sense of her own need for freedom just before she voluntarily re-enters the 'cage' and 'trap' of her marriage to Phillotson. Animals in the novel are usually exploited by man; the cries of the muti-lated rabbit bring Sue and Jude out on a common act of mercy and allow Sue to illustrate how she is hurt and broken by her marriage. The cabhorse kicked at the doors of the Christminster college shows how learning does not automatically lead to compassion and understanding.

In this carefully designed novel, symbols are repeated at intervals: there is, for example, an ever-present policeman, the typical guardian of public morality. He lies in wait for Jude as he reads on his baker's rounds, warns Jude of vagrancy and drunkenness, observes Sue among the roses at the Agricultural Show and emerges from the shadows for the last time after Jude's suicidal journey to Marygreen. Society, we understand, has decided that Jude is its marked victim.

Symbolism can point to similarities between characters, as in the dreamlike episode when Sue, dripping from her flight across the river, has to put on a suit of Jude's clothes. At one stroke she identifies herself as the emotional and imaginative twin of her cousin and his more spiritual self (it is his Sunday suit, not his work clothing). The unlikelihood of such an event is submerged in the symbolic richness of the occasion, and Hardy tactfully dwells on Sue's fevered chill which explains the heightened emotion.

The real imaginative strength of *Jude* seems to lie in the integrity of Hardy's vision. His characters may yearn for the ideal and the spiritual and live in a world of ideas, but the universe that shapes them is real enough, filled with shapes and smells and colours and details that impress themselves on the mind even as we take in the intellectual argument. The stale cakes arranged in the baker's window, Sue's thumb cocked jauntily up her sunshade as she goes unthinkingly to her doom, the beads encrusting Arabella's dress, the creaking weather-vane on the church, the ham that Sue prosaically eats before deserting her husband: such imaginative richness helps us see *Jude the Obscure* as a celebration of the texture of life as well as a sombre vision of intellectual disappointment. Hardy's enthusiastic use of symbolism is always tempered by his sense of the way objects actually appear and his wish to convey precisely the circumstances of his characters' daily lives. Nowhere is this more powerful than in the appalling discovery of the little bodies in the cupboard; what could in other hands have been the crudest melodrama becomes deeply moving as Hardy's eye travels about the room, dwelling on the banal objects that belonged to lives now ended.

The major and minor characters

Jude Fawley

Jude Fawley is linked by Hardy to the grandest and the humblest aspects of human life. At one level he is a baker's boy and later a simple workman; at another, a modern Christ, mysteriously born and fostered in an obscure village, a humble craftsman, a teacher not recognised by the authorities of his day, a moralist and a preacher and a sacrifice to human blindness and folly. The romantic Sue adds to the mystical aura which surrounds Jude; he is to her 'Joseph the dreamer of dreams, a tragic Don Quixote' giving up his life in pursuit of a chivalric ideal, and the martyr St Stephen who saw heaven open to him as he died. Jude has no such final vision of reward; he is named for the saint who watches over lost causes. Hardy himself sees Jude in terms of the human heroes of the Bible: Job who suffered and Samson who was destroyed by the love of women. In his ordinariness, Jude becomes the spokesman for countless inarticulate men and women, yet his relationship to the great heroes of tragedy shows his capacity for greatness. We may also reflect that Michelangelo, perhaps the greatest artist who ever lived, was also a stonemason. Finally, Hardy draws some tentative parallels between the early stages of his own life and that of Jude; Jude is not a self-portrait, but Hardy seems fascinated by the circumstances which could have prevented his becoming a worldly success.

Jude has no reason to have a very good opinion of himself, since his life is such a failure in outward terms. We have to observe his actions and his motives as Hardy interprets them to realise that he is not the 'idle scamp' and 'man with a bad character' he fears he is. Only Sue gives him adequate praise for his 'generous devotion'; otherwise he is mocked as a poor man and a fool by Arabella, the villagers and his low-life cronies. Jude's narrow view of religion has built on his aunt's and Farmer Troutham's criticisms to produce a painfully sensitive conscience; he believes he is full of 'suppressed vices' with 'the germs of every human infirmity' in him. As he tries to rise above his lowly origins, he fears that the vices of the poorer class—strong drink and sexual promiscuity—will show themselves in him, but Hardy assures us that Jude is by nature a temperate man. He gets drunk only as an escape from 'intolerable misery of mind' and shows unusual restraint with the nervous Sue who lives with him on the chastest terms. Jude is 'a strict and formal person' and 'an order loving man' rather than the enemy of society he could easily appear. He has the instincts of a gentleman despite his lowly birth, and protects those weaker than himself: women, children, animals. It is sad, given these fine qualities, to see him convinced that he is a bad man. As his misfortunes crowd in upon him, Jude is forced to give up his 'neat stock of fixed opinions' and is left in 'a chaos of principles' where he can only follow his instincts. That narrow piety which had hidden his own fine nature from him drops away and Jude becomes a cautious, kindly, humane individual who sees the universe as indifferent to man. Human relationships themselves become our only consolation:

> I doubt if I have anything more for my present rule of life than following inclinations which do me and nobody else any harm, and actually give pleasure to those I love best. (6.I)

Jude's is a fine nature warped by the ugliest form of Victorian Christianity. His essential innocence is stressed throughout by Hardy's insistence on his 'childlike' frankness and impulsiveness.

Sue Bridehead

In the character of Jude, Hardy wisely concentrates on the simplicity of his hero and his role as a modern Everyman. The more complex strands of Jude's personality are picked up and woven into his imaginative twin, Sue Bridehead. Much of what we can say of Sue is true of Jude as well, and Hardy has the cousins communicate by a kind of telepathy: 'every glance and movement was as effective as speech for conveying intelligence between them'. In their 'complete mutual understanding' they are 'almost the two parts of a single whole'. This is what the philosopher Plato meant by 'love'.

Sue's name is symbolic: 'Susanna' means 'lily', the symbol of purity, and 'Bridehead' suggests both 'maidenhead' or virginity, and 'bride'. Her nature is likewise both warm and cold, passionate and frigid. Hardy produces an absorbing study of a woman we could judge to be mentally unbalanced if we did not understand her so perfectly. Sue causes two men to die and nearly ruins Phillotson. Yet we pity her because she understands her own strange nature and can do nothing to change it. Her unsureness of herself, her 'love of being loved', make her desperate to have men in love with her. She feels anguish for her victim but is too self-obsessed to give herself to him as a lover. Her virginity is precious to her; she tells Jude proudly that 'I have remained as I began', which is a curiously self-absorbed way of explaining chastity. Sue will not allow herself to change because she cannot admit that she is wrong in any way; even the contradiction of a pet theory reduces her to terror: 'Don't crush all the life out of me by satire and argument!' Eventually her vanity and self-obsession create an imaginary God who is exclusively concerned with Sue's soul, and she destroys Jude in the grotesque worshipping of an idol of her creation.

Sue's chastity is not a natural sign of moral integrity. It is a deeply ingrained vanity, a fear of allowing another person to encroach on her life. It is easy to take Sue either as a study in sexual peculiarity or as a heartless flirt (Gillingham calls her 'a little hussy'), and we have excellent reasons for disliking her if we list all her faults on paper. However it is improbable that many readers do reject her, since Hardy conveys her positive characteristics—her charm, intelligence and vulnerability—so poignantly. Her ideas and her understanding of books are not destined to make her morally strong, since they grow like fragile plants from the soil of her emotions; Jude learns his religious scepticism from harsh experience, whereas Sue's fashionable doubts about the existence of God are a legacy from her love affair in London. Sue's emotionalism and caprice, her 'colossal inconsistency', save her from too much blame even if she does more damage in the course of the novel than the outright villainess, Arabella. Like Jude, Sue is a perpetual child, with a child's craving for love and attention and an ignorance of long-term consequences. 'I crave to get back to the life of my infancy and its freedom', she explains.

Hardy throws most of the blame for Sue's destructive effect on men on to male sexuality; a view of things we may not share. Phillotson and Jude quite reasonably object to Sue's expecting to live with them as a sister, but each comes independently to the conclusion that Sue is too highly developed a moral being to be thought of as a wife. All she can admit to in the way of love, even to Jude, is 'a delight in being with you, of a supremely delicate kind.' It is to Hardy's credit that he refuses to moralise over the sexually impoverished relationship Sue and Jude establish in their years of wandering. His insistence on the tenderness and mutual kindness that grows up between them shows that even the strangest arrangements, if adopted out of love, are valuable consolations for this trouble-filled life.

Arabella Donn

Arabella is very evidently the reverse of the 'divine' Sue, and a symbol of those base qualities of lustfulness that Jude fears he possesses. Her name suggests that 'instinct towards artificiality' which is in her blood: decent country girls are Tess, or Anny, or Marty. Her family name twists the knife in Jude's ruined ambitions, since she is a 'Don(n)' like the teachers in colleges. Hardy cannot resist piling up the evidence against her: she is 'not worth a great deal as a specimen of womankind', her word is 'absolutely untrustworthy', and she has 'no more sympathy than a tigress' with Jude or anybody else. Even her looks are criticised; she begins as 'a fine dark-eyed girl', but is soon dismissed as 'a complete and substantial female animal', becomes 'fleshy' and 'frowsy' in her life of gin-selling and amateur prostitution, and finally is spoken of as a side of bacon sold by her father ('a little bit thick in the flitch'). She is not only a very bad woman in an individual way but she brings with her echoes of the ancient enchantress Circe in the Greek literature Jude reads, who turned men into pigs by offering them liquor and sex. Hardy has a Shakespearean echo in mind as well; Arabella urging Jude to use the knife on his poor 'fellow-mortal', the pig is very like the wicked Lady Macbeth offering her husband a dagger to kill his guest, King Duncan. The case against Arabella seems complete, but Hardy turns the tables on us by showing that in many ways she resembles Sue and Jude. Like her husband she wants to 'improve her circumstances and lead a genteel life', though she intends to do it by running a gin-shop rather than learning Greek. She can be very generous when it suits her, and she refuses to be a 'creeping hypocrite' in her pleasures, just as Jude refuses the appearance of respectability. Like Sue, Arabella turns to religion as a cure for bereavement and melancholy but she gives it up after a comically brief flirtation with self-denial. Her open greed and self-interest is a coarse reproach to the refinement of the lovers, whom she sees as a pair of fools. She cuts through moral ambiguities with a meat-cleaver: 'He'll shake down, they always do.' 'Decency is decency, any hour of the twenty-four.' 'Life with a man is more businesslike after . . . and money-matters work better.' This is not in keeping with Hardy's own moral sensitivity, but it is necessary and refreshing after the paralysed decencies of Sue and Jude. Arabella is much needed comic relief, with her optional dimples and her tail of false hair flung over the looking-glass, her imaginary respectability as the bigamous wife of a publican, and her virtuous rejection of Sue. If we have the heart for such things, her visit of condolence to her former husband after the death of her child is cruelly funny. Arabella is splendidly, laughably, horribly wicked, like the villain in the Christmas mummers' plays, burlesque country dramas of the battle between good and evil, that Hardy watched in his boyhood, and her coarse worldly wisdom counterbalances the sensitivity of Jude and Sue.

Richard Phillotson

The betrayed husband is often a figure of fun, and Phillotson at first seems dull and faded. Yet he becomes a minor masterpiece of character-isation, his sad story underlining Jude's failed hopes, and showing how a basically good man is either warped or destroyed by the pressures of society. Phillotson is a Jude who learns cunning and accepts the values of his fellow men after his frightful experience of social rejection when he lets Sue go.

His name suggests that typical middle-class Victorian ridiculed by the poet and critic Matthew Arnold (1822–1888). Phillotson suggests the 'Philistine' with his petty social ambitions, fear of censure, and ignorance of poetry and refinement. Yet Phillotson proves to be surprisingly sensitive; he is romantically in love with Sue and he has a passion for the past. There is 'a certain gentlemanliness' about him which is in fact a disadvantage in his profession. Schoolteaching in Victorian England was not stimulating; the schoolmaster was meant to be an impossibly precise model of good conduct at the expense of his own spontaneous feeling. When Phillotson allows his unhappy wife to leave he is supposed morally unfit to teach, and is dismissed from his work as quickly as the drunken Jude was turned from the stone-yard. One of the strangest and most moving scenes in the novel is the episode where Sue and Phillotson exchange notes from their separate class-rooms while drilling their charges in learning by heart; a sensitive example of individual feeling set against social conformity.

Phillotson's private character is an attractive one. He has 'an inherent wish to do right by all', is 'kind and considerate', 'manly', 'chivalrous', 'dignified' and 'merciful': all things we could say of Jude. Like Jude, he prides himself on being 'a feeler, not a reasoner' and shares Jude's awe at the sparkling intellect of Sue. When the 'sedate, plodding fellow' as Gillingham calls him suddenly reverses his course and frees his wife we feel that the action is truly noble; we are distressed when weakness of will causes him to entrap her a second time. He is not a villain but a victim of his passion for Sue and his crippling profession; another kind of Jude, but one who decides to survive by adopting the methods of his world.

George Gillingham

Just as we have become entirely absorbed in the emotional tension between Jude, Sue and Phillotson, Gillingham is introduced to give us the outsider's point of view: the plain man's opinion of such reckless goings-on. His attitude is the one which the ordinary reader probably brings to the novel, but Hardy forces us to change our worldly wisdom for a more sympathetic understanding of the central characters. Gillingham is essentially coarse-minded: he ignores the subtleties of Sue's predicament which Hardy has been at pains to present; he believes that Sue 'should be smacked and brought to her senses', which is a better-bred version of Arabella's famous claim that 'there's nothing like bondage and a stone-deaf task-master for taming us women'. At the end of the novel Gillingham has no respect for Phillotson's attempts to behave sensitively, and can only remind him of the social position he has lost. Yet Gillingham is needed in the scheme of the novel as the one person to whom Phillotson can talk candidly—he is a boyhood friend—and to present the attitudes of normal society.

Miss Fawley and the Widow Edlin

Each of these characters keeps us in touch with the roots from which Sue and Jude spring. Jude's aunt is a deeply unlikable old character whose horizons stretch no further than her mouldering breadshop, and she harps continually on Jude's doom-laden future. She tells the stories of hanged, suicidal or absconding Fawleys with enthusiasm, and reminds us that the family is on its way down in the world; Jude's descent into total obscurity is part of an unstoppable process. Every time Jude journeys back to the dying old woman we are reminded how reasonable he is in his wish to escape this narrow world of the gloating, animated old corpse with her 'eyelids heavy as pot-lids' and her vindictive hatred of her adopted Sue.

The Widow Edlin is a somewhat sentimentally portrayed old peasant who shows us the more generous side of rural life. She treats the fine-spun moral debates of Sue and Jude with a hearty contempt, and is much needed in the scheme of the novel as a go-between once Sue has left Jude for Phillotson, and between Sue and her husband to underline our awareness of his deliberate cruelty in taking her back against her will. She is one of the speakers over the dead body of Jude; a woman who is near the end of her life and who has survived so long because she has never questioned her values.

Little Father Time

Young Jude is a character so purely symbolic as to be hardly believable in ordinary terms. He may be partly Arabella's, but his inheritance is pure Fawley. 'Little Father Time' is introduced in a splendid long passage, refusing to laugh with the others at the antics of a kitten on the train, and setting off like a robot Nemesis or agent of fate towards Jude's lodging at 'a slow mechanical creep.' Young Jude is his father without Jude's redeeming qualities of ambition, sexual vitality and the ability to enter imaginatively into other people's feelings. The boy is introduced to bring about the catastrophe of the novel when he hangs himself and his half-brother and sister. Jude as a child 'did not want to be a man' and sought for a way to 'prevent himself growing up.' His son succeeds in this melancholy ambition.

Part 4

Hints for study

A guide to reading the novel

As you read *Jude the Obscure* keep a pen in your hand and underline or mark those passages which seem to you particularly significant, with a view to framing answers in class or in essays. Check in particular those passages in which Hardy pauses in his story to tell you what he thinks of the characters and their situation. Mark passages which seem to you especially rich in *imagery*; they are very likely *symbolic* of the characters' predicament at that moment. For example, when Jude looks down the well in that superb passage at the end of the first chapter, he is metaphorically responding to the fatal pull of the past and going down into the darkness of the grave at the same time that Hardy poignantly catches the beauty of the fleeting moment. Think about following the various symbolic themes through the novel; for example, Hardy's use of darkness, light, fog and mist to suggest the error and bewilderment in which his characters move. Other symbols you may consider include animals (the pigs that are associated with Jude's baser nature and the birds that are linked to Sue, the free spirit), ghosts (Sue and Jude become more and more wraith-like as their fate works itself out) and crossroads, symbolising choices made and paths taken. Your pen should be in constant use, because a well-marked copy of the text is a sign that you are reading intelligently and preparing conscientiously for written work.

Take note of those passages which show Hardy's *irony*, when the characters misinterpret events, miss appointments or meet by mischance. Think of how Sue and Jude greet Little Time with such happiness and optimism, and what an appalling effect the child has on them. Remember that one of the key questions in the novel asks how much freedom of will the characters have. Could they have acted differently if they had wanted to, or does Hardy show them acting under some inner compulsion? Look at the point where Sue and Jude turn to one another and passionately kiss before Sue goes back to her husband. This is the main *turning point* of a novel filled with new beginnings which in fact only serve to make Jude's defeat more inevitable.

How do you react to the *bizarre events* of the novel? How probable is it that Sue should worship images of pagan gods in her room? Is it likely that married schoolteachers would spend a whole day arguing the ethics of marriage in notes exchanged in front of classes? How does Hardy make this sort of improbable incident not only believable in terms of the lives of his characters, but resonant with emotion?

Every time you come across a reference to the *character* of one of the principal figures, mark it down and take note of who is speaking. Build up a list of personality traits for each character. You may be surprised to find that Hardy spends twice as much time defining Sue's character as he does Jude's. Does this suggest that he was really writing a novel about Sue Bridehead? Some critics think he was.

You will notice that *coincidence* plays a large, indeed almost extravagant part in the novel. Arabella in particular makes a habit of being in the wrong place at the wrong time throughout, and her presence forces Jude, Sue or Phillotson to take the steps which their lack of initiative prevents them from taking for themselves. Arabella almost runs the plot single-handed, but her presence is usually the result of blind chance. Some critics think that this habit of moving the plot along by chance meetings is a cheap device forced on Hardy by his habit of writing for serial publication, which meant that exciting confrontations and changes of plot had to occur very frequently. Other critics argue that each human life is ruled by coincidence and Hardy's novels merely imitate reality; at the same time, Hardy emphasises the unusually bad luck that follows Jude and Sue to impress on us the folly of their optimism. If things can go wrong, they will.

Look into the instances of *conflict* within the novel; just as Nature's law, according to Sue, is 'mutual butchery', so it is impossible for one character to follow his own interest without harming another. When Jude claims that he is not 'a man who wants to save himself at the expense of the weaker' he explains the cause of his downfall; Hardy believes in the survival of the fittest, who are rarely the finest, morally speaking. Arabella achieves her goal of marriage by making Jude sacrifice his hopes of an education; Sue, Jude and Phillotson cannot resolve their conflicting desires; Phillotson at the end of the novel decides to save himself by breaking Sue's spirit and robbing Jude of the will to live. We see the idea of conflict continued in the way in which characters no sooner escape from a bad situation than they find themselves in a worse; all of Sue and Jude's desperate wanderings bring them back to Christminster, the most dismal place of all. Sue escapes from her life of drudgery at the inquisitive Miss Fontover's only to find herself engaged to Phillotson and a greater prisoner than ever in the Training School. Jude does his cousin a favour by finding her work that suits her talents, and discovers that he has offered her to a rival in love. The more the characters struggle to free themselves, the more they are maimed and broken, like the rabbit in the trap at Marygreen.

Look at the *setting* of the novel, following the guidelines given earlier (pp. 52-4). Notice how the various locations give us different emotional sensations, and in particular see how Christminster becomes more and more menacing until it is seen through the gloomy imagination of Little Time as a place of death and judgement. See how often people change their dwellings, and how this detaches them from any sense of stability or permanent affection. 'Out o'doors in all season and weathers—lovers and homeless dogs only', says a countryman contemptuously early in the novel; *Jude* is filled with vagrants such as Vilbert and the fairground people, and Sue and Jude become homeless wanderers across Wessex.

Finally, look at the *shape* of the novel. What is the effect of our early discovery that Jude is destined to remain 'obscure' and will never enter a Christminster college? Notice the perfect reversal by which the pious Jude and the unbelieving Sue exchange roles. There is a crisis at the halfway point where the cousins admit their unlawful love and act upon it, and a catastrophe where the children are found dead. How does Hardy deal with the aftermath of this disaster, and how well has he prepared you for this most memorable chapter of the novel?

Key quotations to guide your interpretation

These half-dozen passages sum up the central themes of the novel; you will find others to supplement them, but each paragraph quoted will bear a great deal of careful analysis. Hardy makes every image, every clause count.

(1) Jude went out, and feeling more than ever his existence to be an undemanded one, he lay down upon his back on a heap of litter near the pigsty. The fog had by this time become more translucent, and the position of the sun could be seen through it. He pulled his straw hat over his face, and peered through the interstices of the plaiting at the white brightness, vaguely reflecting. Growing up brought responsibilities, he found. Events did not rhyme quite as he had thought. Nature's logic was too horrid for him to care for. That mercy towards one set of creatures was cruelty towards another sickened his sense of harmony. As you got older, and felt yourself to be at the centre of your time, and not at a point on its circumference, as you had felt when you were little, you were seized with a sort of

shuddering, he perceived. All around you there seemed something glaring, garish, rattling, and the noises and glares hit upon the little cell called your life, and shook it, and warped it.

If only he could prevent himself growing up! He did not want to be a man. (1.II)

This passage, which occurs just after Jude has been beaten by Farmer Troutham, establishes that the foundations of Jude's tragedy lie in his own character. Both Jude and Sue wish to stay childlike forever; impulsive, emotional and idealistic. It is typical of Jude when he discovers that the business of Nature is the mere survival of one's own kind at the expense of others, that he makes up his mind that this is 'too horrid for him to care for' and ignores it. Hardy produces a superb prose-poem of a child's soul trapped in rattling machinery as external forces combine to crush it. We think of Jude as a victim of his industrial century, and also of Little Time later in his railway carriage. In this passage Hardy characteristically plays off the 'real'—the pigsty—against the 'ideal', the white fog which symbolises the imaginative nature of Jude and his longings for that 'city of light', Christminster.

(2) For a moment there fell on Jude a true illumination; that here in the stone yard was a centre of effort as worthy as that dignified by the name of scholarly study within the noblest of the colleges. But he lost it under stress of his old idea. He would accept any employment which might be offered him on the strength of his late employer's recommendation; but he would accept it as a provisional thing only. That was his form of the modern vice of unrest.

Moreover he perceived that at best only copying, patching and imitating went on here; which he fancied to be owing to some temporary and local cause. He did not at that time see that medievalism was as dead as a fernleaf in a lump of coal; that other developments were shaping the world around him, in which Gothic architecture and its associations had no place. The deadly animosity of contemporary logic and vision towards so much of what he held in reverence was not yet revealed to him. (2.II)

Hardy is aware, as Jude is not, that the life of a skilled craftsman who understands every branch of his art is a noble thing. He sees Jude's obsession with Christminster as a form of 'the modern vice of unrest', a theory he returns to several times in the novel, and in particular during Jude's Remembrance Day 'sermon'. Hardy has a complex view of social change; he was well aware of the brutish poverty and immorality of country dwellers, hinted at in the circumstances which surround

Jude's first marriage, but never described fully for fear people would reject such coarse realism. In general, Hardy thought that the life of the poorest members of the community had been immeasurably improved in his lifetime. But the price for this was a general rootlessness. Jude and Sue have no links with a family, a place, or a class, and inhabit a frightening social and spiritual solitude. 'Gothic architecture', a prevailing symbol in the novel, is a metaphor for a form of society like that of Europe in the Middle Ages, centred on the worship of God, spirituality preferred to material progress, and the community rigorously controlled by the lords of church and state. Christminster still seeks to preserve this entrenched system of privilege; Hardy sees the Middle Ages as a time to be rejected.

(3) Half an hour later they all lay in their cubicles, their tender feminine faces upturned to the flaring gas-jets which at intervals stretched down the long dormitories, every face bearing the legend 'The Weaker' upon it, as the penalty of the sex wherein they were moulded, which by no possible exception of their willing hearts and abilities could be made strong while the inexorable laws of nature remain what they are. They formed a pretty, suggestive, pathetic little sight, of whose pathos and beauty they were themselves unconscious, and would not discover till, amid the storms and strains of after-years, with their injustice, loneliness, child-bearing, and bereavement, their minds would revert to this experience as to something which had been allowed to slip past them insufficiently regarded. (3.III)

This is Hardy at his best; scarcely another passage in the novel touches this for intelligent and sad reflection. Hardy is really writing about the absent Sue Bridehead, in that we apply these words to her in particular as her tragedy works itself out. He illustrates how impossible it is to take an optimisitic view of life when tragedy grows so naturally out of our biological existence; women are born to be broken by marriage and childbirth. This passage shows what good use Hardy makes of his powers as an ominiscient narrator, showing us the gloomy after-years of these girls' lives and the glow that memory will cast on their deprived adolescence.

(4) . . . He only heard in part the policeman's further remarks, having fallen into thought on what struggling people like himself had stood at that Crossway, whom nobody ever thought of now. It had more history than the oldest College in the city. It was literally teeming, stratified, with the shades of human groups, who had met there for tragedy, comedy, farce; real enactments of the intensest kind. At

Fourways men had stood and talked of Napoleon, the loss of America, the execution of King Charles, the burning of the Martyrs, the Crusades, the Norman Conquest, possibly of the arrival of Caesar. Here the two sexes had met for loving, hating, coupling, parting; had waited, had suffered, for each other; had triumphed over each other; cursed each other in jealousy, blessed each other in forgiveness. (2.VI)

If the former passage (3) shows how Hardy believes that the individual life tends towards disappointment and tragedy, this one shows how his novels avoid dire pessimism. Hardy is gifted at showing how multiple layers of human lives build up like strata in the earth's crust, and no emotion felt is ever quite dispelled. Sometimes we feel, like Sue, the oppressive weight of so many dead lives, but here the impression is one of vitality and sympathy. If *Jude the Obscure* has a final positive meaning, it is Hardy's insistence on the value of 'obscure' lives which are not without valuable private joys and sorrows.

(5) Strange that his first aspiration—towards academical proficiency—had been checked by a woman, and that his second aspiration—towards apostleship—had also been checked by a woman. 'Is it,' he said, 'that the women are to blame; or is it the artificial system of things, under which normal sex-impulses are turned into devilish domestic gins and springes to noose and hold back those who want to progress?' (4.III)

We have seen in (3) how Hardy believed that nature was particularly cruel to women. Here we see the similar problem that faces men; their hopes of bettering their own and others' lives are destroyed by the sexual instinct. Neither Jude nor Hardy answers his hero's question, but there is the gloomy suggestion that the sex instinct is a black joke of nature's; misery is perpetuated generation after generation, Job is right to curse the day of his birth, and human beings in love are like the coupling earthworms beneath a boy's feet.

(6) 'It was my poverty and not my will that consented to be beaten. It takes two or three generations to do what I tried to do in one; and my impulses—affections—vices perhaps they should be called—were too strong not to hamper a man without advantages; who should be as cold-blooded as a fish and as selfish as a pig to have a good chance of being one of his country's worthies. You may ridicule me—I am quite willing that you should—I am a fit subject, no doubt. But I think that if you knew what I have gone through these last few years you would rather pity me.' (6.I)

Jude shows how qualities lurking in his own nature have brought about his tragic downfall. Yet Hardy stresses an element of social satire in the novel at this point. When Jude lies dead in the final chapter, students are cheering a Duke who has bought himself an honorary degree though he may have less Greek and Latin than Jude had. Hardy does not deny his hatred of a class system which refused advancement to the gifted poor, but he intelligently refuses to make his social criticism the centre of his novel. He knew people would be reading it even after men from Jude's background were admitted to universities without question.

The handling of essay or examination topics

(1) Discuss the way Hardy uses the setting to establish the themes of *Jude the Obscure*.

If you approach the novel *chronologically*, that is, episode by episode, you will end by producing a clear picture of the way Jude's history darkens and Hardy's tragic theme is made obvious. Hardy is not producing a simple vision of the countryside as wholesome and the city as destructive; qualities are always mixed. The changes in Marygreen demonstrate the breakdown of old rural values and the shepherd's country near Wardour Castle the impossibility of getting back to them. Towns and cities tend to elaborate and symbolise qualities in their inhabitants: Shaston is like Phillotson, Melchester like Sue, Christminster as forbidding as the heads of its colleges. A town may contain warring elements; the colleges and slums of Christminster suggest the physical and spiritual impulses in Jude himself. Think of the reasons why characters move from place to place. What is Hardy saying about our need to belong somewhere?

(2) 'The character of Sue is considerably more complex than that of Jude: the novel is in fact more about her strange nature than Jude's fall.' Discuss.

As usual, there are no right or wrong answers to such a question; merely well and less well argued responses. A very good case can be made out for Sue's central place in the novel. She is one of the first women in fiction to have had her private sexual history so carefully and sympathetically documented. Hardy has a liking for his heroine which readers may not share, but he is careful to show her faults as well as her charm. You could point out that Hardy takes more pains to describe Sue than he does over Jude; she is more of an individual and less of a symbolic victim. Yet on the other hand Sue is designed to exaggerate qualities present in Jude; his intellect, his childishness, his idealism. *Jude the Obscure* is named after its hero, not its heroine, and if we take Sue as the central character we are left with the story of a human being who is utterly destroyed and whom we abandon to her errors.

(3) '*Jude the Obscure* is based upon a series of contrasts of characters, setting and moral qualities.' Show how Hardy uses such opposites in the construction of this novel.

This is a useful question for a well-prepared student. Begin by making a quick list on a spare sheet of paper, and then arrange it according to importance or theme. Remember that Hardy bases his novel on the contrast between the real and the ideal, the physical and the spiritual, and the male and the female: these are subdivided into pairs like the flesh and the spirit, marriage and comradeship, poetry and brutish survival, light and darkness, churches and taverns, colleges and slums, Christianity and paganism, ancient country ways and new inventions. The message is always that these opposites cannot be reconciled and that conflict is inevitable in life. You should state in your conclusion that Jude and Sue embody opposite states of mind in the novel, and ironically exchange their attitudes towards the end.

(4) '*Jude the Obscure* is more about feelings than ideas.' Argue for or against this suggestion.

This question goes to the heart of one aspect of the novel; how much was Hardy writing against marriage and the class system? A good student will be careful about the *emphasis* of his answer; of course Hardy is concerned with social injustice, and you will mention those passages where he condemns immoral country habits, lazy or debt-ridden clergymen, the pride of the intellectual élite, women viewed merely as property, social hypocrisy and the sale of university degrees. Hardy uses satire against these curable follies and vices. But even if these faults could be removed, we are left with the great problem of Nature's indifference as she uses suffering men and women as the blind instruments of generation. Also, if Hardy sees social injustice as a scientific necessity, man's way of selecting the toughest and fittest of his species to produce more of their own kind, there is not much we can do about it. The emphasis in the novel is on the inevitability and the pity of Jude and Sue's tragedy; the very qualities that make them admirable cause them to lose the battle for survival.

(5) Critics often argue that Little Time is a failure as a character. How would you defend his place in the novel?

Hardy introduces this strange child in a passage almost unequalled for gloomy and detailed physical observation, but it must be admitted that he scarcely knows what to do with the boy until the time comes to destroy the children. We could argue more positively that we add what we know of Jude as a child to what we see of his son by Arabella, to make one fully developed character. (It is usually a safe principle to look for strengths rather than weaknesses in the work under consideration.) In an obvious sense, Little Time illustrates the curse that hangs over married Fawleys and the blind way in which individuals seeking a way out of a particular trap manage to find their way into a worse. Little Time cannot understand the central 'riddle' of existence—the mystery of human conception—and takes upon himself the blame for there being too many children. Hardy saves some of his finest effects for the flesh-crawling scene with the kitten in the railway carriage, the 'slow mechanical creep' of the doomladen child to Jude's house, and the appalling page where the bodies of the children are discovered. You have to decide whether the emotional power of the catastrophe is worth the limitations of the character.

(6) Compare and contrast the roles of Arabella and Phillotson.

Any question involving Arabella and Phillotson is a good choice for an essay. Both characters are fascinating mixtures of good and bad qualities. Hardy sets out to make Arabella a monster, but in spite of her grotesque selfishness she is a necessary contrast to the spiritual Sue. Phillotson, psychologically crippled by his fear of losing his right to teach and much older than the other characters, is both victim and torturer. He is Jude's rival, but like Jude in many significant ways; his ambition, his love of Sue, his sensuality. Both spouses undergo a change of heart along with the hero and heroine; Arabella parodies Sue's religious conversion in her brief episode of chapel-going, and Phillotson, like Jude, briefly becomes a spokesman for social outcasts. Arabella and Phillotson are successful in worldly terms while Sue and Jude are destroyed; Arabella, we feel, is morally worthless and Phillotson is a good man destroyed by social disapproval. He does not have the courage of a Jude to bear the weight of the world's anger when he follows his conscience.

(7) In what sense can *Jude the Obscure* be called a tragedy?

Hardy believed in the classical Greek idea of tragedy, and has Sue and Jude compare their situation to the story of Agamemnon at various points. According to this theory, a man better than most of us but still possessing weaknesses that make him human rather than saintly undertakes a grand project but is destroyed in pursuit of it by a crucial flaw in his character. It is usually arranged that his hopes are overturned to have their opposite effect, through the hidden operations of fate, and in the fall of the hero his whole family is brought to ruin. Jude's weakness for women and liquor makes him human, and his idealism and compassion are the 'weaknesses' which destroy him. Yet Hardy goes beyond the prescriptions of narrow classical theories of tragedy; Jude is no king or hero but a simple man, and his story is set in the context of perpetual human disappointment and the indifference of an amoral universe.

Part 5

Suggestions for further reading

The text

The best annotated edition of the text for students is the New Wessex Edition of *Jude the Obscure*, Macmillan, London, 1974, with notes and an introduction by Terry Eagleton.

Biography

The best biography of Hardy is the recent two-volume study by Robert Gittings: *Young Thomas Hardy* and *The Older Hardy*, published in London in 1975 and 1978 respectively. It is also worth consulting *The Life of Thomas Hardy* by Hardy's second wife, Florence Emily Hardy; this curious book was written as a third person autobiography by Hardy himself and his wife added only four last chapters and a few corrections. This 'biography' of Hardy was published originally as *The Early Life of Thomas Hardy* in 1928 and *The Later Years of Thomas Hardy* in 1930; they were published as a single volume in 1962.

Criticism

The best critical text is J.I.M. Stewart's *Thomas Hardy: a critical biography*, London, 1971. The life of Hardy is considered in relation to his novels; an elegant, thought-provoking study which also assesses other critics' opinions.

The author of these notes

MARGARET STONYK took her first degree at the University of Adelaide, South Australia, in 1967, and received her Ph.D. from the University of Leeds in 1970 for a thesis on William Morris and Victorian poetry. She has taught at universities in Australia and Canada, and was a lecturer at the University of Stirling in Scotland for three years. She has published articles on poetry and the fine arts in the nineteenth century and contributed a chapter to a volume of studies on Victorian poetry. Dr Stonyk is at work currently on a book surveying the art of biography.